Between Friends

A novel by
Keith O'Brien

Global Learning Systems, LLC
FORT LAUDERDALE, FL 33301

© 2000 Keith O'Brien. Printed and bound in the United States of America. All rights reserved. No part of this book may be reproduced or transmitted in any form or by any means, electronic or mechanical, including photocopying, recording, or by an information storage and retrieval system—except by a reviewer who may quote brief passages in a review to be printed in a magazine or newspaper—without permission in writing from the publisher. For information, please contact Global Learning Systems, LLC, 1314 E. Las Olas Blvd., #15, Fort Lauderdale, FL 33301.

Although the author and publisher have made every effort to ensure the accuracy and completeness of information contained in this book, we assume no responsibility for errors, inaccuracies, omissions, or any inconsistency herein. Any slights of people, places, or organizations are unintentional.

First printing 2000

ISBN 0-9679394-4-5

LCCN 00 130978

ATTENTION CORPORATIONS, UNIVERSITIES, COLLEGES, AND PROFESSIONAL ORGANIZATIONS: Quantity discounts are available on bulk purchases of this book for educational purposes. Special books or book excerpts can also be created to fit specific needs. For information, please contact Global Learning Systems, LLC, 1314 E. Las Olas Blvd., #15, Fort Lauderdale, FL 33301; phone 954-522-2696.

ACKNOWLEDGMENTS

I suppose I could begin by thanking God, but that is so cliché. It would be appropriate, but nonetheless, it's still a cliché. I think the world's a bit tired, at least I know I am, of hearing every athlete and famous person speak about themselves in the third person when being interviewed, and thank God for everything they have accomplished.

I once heard a comedian do a bit on why no one ever blamed God when they lost a big game. Imagine an NFL football player in a post-game interview saying, "You know, we had it, the game was ours, and I would have caught that touchdown pass with three seconds left. But God made me drop it." Seriously, although I absolutely and unequivocally believe God consciousness is the source of all power, I think He/She knows very clearly that I've acknowledged Him/Her all along.

So let's move on to the people who have played an important role in assisting me in the process of writing this book. There is no one! I did it all my damn self! It was me, all me! Oh, but not so. My wonderful sister, Tara O'Brien, was the first person I trusted to read it as it was produced. Tara has been a constant encouraging voice not only for this book but for my life as well. Surely Mom and Dad have been in my corner the entire time. Dad is the proverbial pillar to lean against, and I think Mom was just as excited as I was when the pages started turning out. I must certainly thank Sarah Illingworth, who has given me some incredibly valuable feedback throughout the entire process, both personally and professionally. Sarah has helped keep me in the space necessary to write. She has been the perfect friend at the times when I needed it the most. And to all the great teachers that I have encountered so far throughout my own journey—many of whom are still very close and dear friends—I cherish your wisdom, I embrace your spirit, and I am grateful for your willingness to share your insights, your passions, and your visions.

Most of all, I want to thank life itself for being such a wonderful episode of pleasures and challenges. I want to thank the fact that I didn't learn too quickly and that I was able to make many fantastic mistakes along the way—and still am. Although I refer to them as mistakes, they have helped shape my character and my life as much as the successes. From the moment I awake each day to the moment I close my eyes, and all the dream-time in between, I love it all!

CHAPTER ONE

"So what did you and Hope do last night?" Pete asked as he passed the roach clip to Cole.

"Ah, just the normal crap, you know. She made dinner, we watched a video, then we did it like rabbits for about an hour and fell asleep in a sweaty pile." Emmmphf...as Cole took a nice big hit from the joint.

"Did she find out about that chick from Murphy's last weekend?" chimed in Jake.

"Hell no, and she's not going to. Just as long as you keep your damn mouth shut. She didn't talk to me for a week when she overheard you and Pete laughing about that other girl I slept with."

Ever since they were kids, Pete Landry, Cole Anderson, and Jake Nelson had been the best of friends. Although they could trust each other with anything, Jake was a compulsive talker and Cole and Pete knew it. Most of the time it actually made situations more comical than ever. But every now and then, if Jake had a good enough buzz on, he'd let something critical out to the wrong person.

During high school they had been inseparable, and the beginning of college was looking like more of the same.

About the only time they weren't together was when Pete was at baseball practice or when Cole went off with Hope somewhere to have their privacy. All three of them had been athletes in high school, and although both Cole and Pete were good enough to play in college, Cole choose to give up sports when high school was over.

Cole didn't do very well with authority. Although a team player and liked by everyone, he often battled with coaches. He was a free spirit and didn't like to be confined by rules, especially when he didn't see the purpose of the rule. He had an incredible need to question things, not only with his coaches, but with his parents and teachers as well. Pete, although not quite the rebel Cole was, got into his share of disagreements with the coaches. If it weren't for their pure talent, neither one of them would have made it past little league.

"That wasn't my fault, Cole, I didn't know she was listening. How the hell was I suppose to know she was already in the house waiting for you when we walked in?" Jake protested, referring to a night about two months before when Cole had hooked up with some girl after a long night of partying. It was one of those historic Saturday nights when Hope was out of town and the boys, fake IDs in hand, headed over to one of the local campus bars. Southern California State University was a relatively large school only about four hours south of where they had grown up. Although a good school for academics with a more than fair athletic department, SCSU was best known for its extracurricular activities. While in high school they had journeyed down south many times to the SCSU campus to visit older friends who had introduced them to many of the campus's taverns, clubs, and hot spots.

That infamous Saturday night, as the lights in the bar came on to signify the 2:00 A.M. closing time, Cole was putting the finishing touches on the masterpiece of a story he had been building for the last hour with this adorable little blond sophomore. He had never met her before but had bumped into her while coming back from the bathroom. She looked up with her green eyes semi-floating in alcohol and offered a half-witted apology for not watching where she was going. Without skipping a beat, Cole quickly apologized, saying it was entirely his fault, and offered to buy her a drink as a way of making it up to her. One drink turned into another. Then into a walk home. Then into breakfast. The next morning, as Cole got dressed to leave, he couldn't help but think of his girlfriend, Hope. As quickly as the thoughts of guilt entered his mind, he got up, shrugged them off, and left for home.

"It's already been almost two months. How long are you going to keep throwing it back in my face?" Jake shouted, not really looking for an answer. "You've got to admit though, Cole, that story was worth talking about. I mean, it's not every day you can convince someone you're an actor doing research for a movie who is at this college to find out what makes up 'the average student.' I've known ya for a long time, and that was one of the best raps I've ever heard. Pure genius!"

"Yes, I agree." Cole replied swankily as he sat up tall and put his hand between the buttons of his shirt as if he were Napoleon. "All right, Sir-Talk-A-Lot, pass that dube over here and all is forgiven." Emmmphf, as he took another hit. Cole turned to talk to Pete. "So they're working you pretty hard over there in practice, huh?"

"Yeah, you know how the off-season is in baseball. A shitload of running, weights, and drills. Sometimes I wish I had decided not to play at all, like you did. Ah hell, games will start shortly after we get back from the break. And if Coach Numbnuts knows what's good for him," which was Pete's way of referring to any coach he ever had, "I'll be the starting shortstop as a freshman! Oh, yeah!" Emmmphf, Pete took a nice big hit, barely stopping in time to keep from burning his lips. They all high-fived as Pete blew out his hit in a big cloud of smoke.

"Starting varsity b-ball as a fresh has got to be one of the biggest pussy magnets there is—it's like having a Porsche or something. You'll be swimming in it, Pete. Just remember those of us who are a bit more deprived in the getting laid department when you're a campus legend," requested Jake, who—although he was a pretty decent-looking guy—often got nervous around women. For some reason that none of them could figure out, when Jake got really nervous he tended to stutter, which didn't exactly make for the best first impressions.

Neither Pete nor Cole had any trouble with women. In fact, Cole might have even been too good at it. He had been going out with Hope for two and a half years now, but he still couldn't find a way to be faithful. They had dated throughout their last two years in high school and although he felt he loved her, he was only mildly happy when she also decided to go to SCSU. He treated her well, but it was as if he was obsessed with the game. The challenge of getting someone new into bed thrilled him. He could talk with the best of them, and he and Pete often would make a night out of telling the most outrageous stories to unsuspecting women in bars.

Still pretending to be Napoleon, Cole said, "Well, my loyal subjects, I must bid you a fond farewell." Then laughing, he exclaimed, "I've got to split—I've got English starting in ten minutes!"

"Catch ya later, partner," yelled Pete and Jake as the screen door flung shut behind Cole.

Cole was one of those people who had a certain air about him you just had to like. Growing up, he was constantly in trouble, yet managed to always find a way out of actually getting blamed and come out okay. He had a handsome face and boyish charm, and most people found it hard to dislike him for too long. Although he was in all the advanced classes, he was extremely under-challenged. For the most part, Cole found school boring. Since he usually finished his work in less time than most of the other students in class, he had a lot of time on his hands and generally ended up causing some sort of trouble. He had a very special love-hate relationship with a lot of his teachers. They loved that he was bright, intelligent, and witty, but hated that he usually found some way to stir up trouble. He had boundless energy growing up and didn't always find the most productive ways to channel it. He was one of those people who are good at just about everything except, perhaps, pleasing themselves.

"So, you want to go get a fish taco?" asked Jake as he threw on his shirt and started putting on his Nikes.

"You buying?" Pete asked. On their budgets, if either of them was buying, it would only be for some female he was trying to make points with.

"Yeah, right. Not today, not tomorrow! Come on, let's go."

"So what are you doing over Christmas break?" asked Jake. They sat at an outdoor table next to the small, makeshift taco stand. Despite its poor construction, this little appetite oasis was always crowded with hungry students. "Got any plans?" he continued with fish taco lettuce hanging from the corner of his mouth. "Hell, we've got five weeks off."

"Well, we've got to be here almost the whole time for practice, except for the week around Christmas, which really sucks. So I don't have anything big lined up. What about you?" asked Pete.

"You know my family, Pete. Our Christmas is the same every year: 'Hi, how ya doin'? Great! Here's a present. There's the turkey. Okay, I gotta go.' Christmas is nothing special at the Nelson house. But I think I am going to drive down to Cabo with Cole and Hope when finals are done," Jake added.

"Sure, rub it in, you little bastard. I'll be up here sweating my ass off, listening to Coach Numbnuts bark orders at me, and you'll be sipping Coronas and margaritas and getting laid by some little *señorita*. Ah well, like you said, being the starting shortstop will have its advantages. Hey, Jake, look at her!" Pete whispered suddenly, motioning to a girl in the order line. "If those shorts were any shorter, they'd be a belt! She's got ass hanging out all over the place. You know, more women should take her lead; there's nothing like seeing a nice butt on a beautiful day to cheer you up."

Pete, in his usual James Bond style, said, "Excuse me, but I couldn't help notice your fine choice in fashion today. Those shorts are not only functional for this beautiful afternoon, but also show off your incredible figure, if you don't mind my saying."

"Is that so? Well, why don't you get a closer look, just to be sure?" replied the girl as she bent over and virtually stuck her butt in his face. Stunned, Pete sat there with his jaw dropped open, speechless. "See you later, hotshot," remarked the girl as she jumped into her car and drove off.

"What a woman. You know, I could marry a girl like that, Jake. She's got an ass that could stop a tornado and an attitude to go along with it. You've got to love it," Pete said, the visual image of her bending over in front of him still fresh in his mind.

"Yeah, right. That'll be the day—when you get married. Yeah, and Cole's gonna be faithful to Hope, too."

"Shssssh, Jake. Here she comes," Pete said as Hope appeared around the corner.

"Hey, guys, what's up?" Hope said, sitting down to join them.

Hope Stewart was a sincere and genuine girl who was madly in love with Cole. They had all grown up together, with Hope having a crush on Cole for as long as anyone could remember. Although she forgave Cole often, she kept him on his toes. It was as if Hope could look deep inside Cole and truly see not only what he was, but also what he would become. Hope was one of the few people Cole had really opened up to. With Hope he shared his dreams and insecurities, his plans and his fears. In many ways, Cole was closer to her than anyone else in the world.

She was a beautiful, tall, slender young woman of nineteen. Her bright blue eyes sparkled in the sun and her wavy, light brown hair blew gently in the breeze as she sat down to join Jake and Pete. The two guys thought the world of Hope and never minded her hanging around. She was probably the best "girl" friend either of them had ever had. Hope often played counselor to the guys, as they liked to confide their girl problems or family issues to her. The four of them were as tight as you could get and had been for years.

"You want a taco?" Jake asked.

"No, thanks, I've got to go to class. I just stopped by to say 'hi.' We're starting to review today for my history final. Talk about snoozeville! Anyway, I got to run. Tell Cole I'll call him tonight," Hope said as she walked toward campus.

"See ya, girl," they both said as Hope waved without looking back.

"That was close, Jake. You almost blew it again," Pete said, referring to Hope's nearly overhearing Jake's wisecrack.

"Ah, relax. She didn't hear. But you know Cole's gonna get himself busted. You can only play with that for so long. Hope's a fantastic girl. Sometimes I don't know why the hell he just doesn't stay faithful to her," Jake complained.

"Shiiiiiiittttttt. You know Cole. He's addicted to the chase. He loves the challenge. We both do. It's fun. There is just that feeling you get when you are talking to a girl you don't know, and as you're talking, you know that she's yours. It's like you're fucking her already but just with your mind. Mind sex is some serious fun, even though it still doesn't replace the real thing," Pete said as he stood up to leave.

"The real thing? You mean love?" asked Jake.

"No, dumbass...actually having sex. Love! Yeah, right. Who's got the time or the patience for love? Let's get outta here."

"Can't. I've got lab tonight, so I'm gonna head down to campus," Jake said.

"Yeah, all right. Man, I can't wait for break. Only another week of books until a nice, long, well-deserved vacation if I do say so myself. I'll catch ya later, Jake," Pete said and turned to head back to the house.

The last few days rolled by, final exams came and went, and the results were about as they had always been in high school. Hope, who had a knack for studying and actually enjoyed school, did extremely well. Jake, who tended to lose interest quickly in almost anything, scraped the bottom portion of the barrel. And Cole and Pete did exactly as much as they needed to receive the grades they wanted.

As the campus slowed down to a crawl, Hope, Jake, and Cole packed up Cole's Jeep (a graduation present) and headed off down the coast for Cabo San Lucas, Mexico.

CHAPTER TWO

"Go, go, go, go, go," chanted the crowd as Cole tipped his head backward over a chair, while the tequila and margarita mix poured down his throat. Bartenders and waiters were blowing whistles loudly and people all around the bar were cheering and screaming for him to keep going. He flung himself back to a semi-upright position with a loud cough and, smiling brightly, put his hands straight up over his head as if he had just scored a touchdown. That was his fourth upside-down margarita in the last hour. The day was in full swing.

"You sure I'm not being a third wheel, Cole?" Jake asked as he finished chugging his beer.

"Of course not, my bruddha, you're a wheel that fits on this car right where the wheel is supposed to go, dammit. And it fits as much as any wheel that could be on this car or in the trunk or on the back like those old cars," Cole replied, slurring his words.

"Huh?" Jake replied, "what the hell did you say, you drunk bastard?"

"I, ah, I mean…you're not a fifth wheel, or whatever you said. Hope and I can always find time to romp around in the sheets." Cole looked over at Hope and said, "Isn't that right, baby?"

Hope just looked at her intoxicated boyfriend. "Oh, you're so romantic, Cole."

"Hey, you've got to admit sex is the easy part. It's the other stuff that's hard. So anyway, my bruddha, what I was saying is you don't always find time to get drunk in Cabo with your best friends, right?" Cole exclaimed putting one arm around Jake's shoulder and the other around Hope, half intending to show them how much he loved them and half intending to hold himself up.

"*Más cerveza, Señor!*" Cole shouted at the guy behind the bar. "*Très* Coronas, *por favor*. Hey, Hopes, bet you didn't know I was so bilingual, huh? I also can say, 'Where's the toilet?' and 'How much for that?' and 'I am a U.S. Senator—leave me alone.' Yes indeed, Hopes, your man can speak in many tongues."

"*That* I knew," laughed Hope, and they all burst into hysterical laughter. Jake wasn't sure if that meant Hope knew how much Cole could bullshit or whether he could do amazing things with his tongue. He decided, either way, it was pretty funny.

The evening sun went down and the day melted into night. The sunset in Cabo San Lucas is absolutely incredible. Cabo is a small-but-never-quiet little Mexican town about eight hundred or so miles south of San Diego. The climate is much like that of San Diego but a little warmer. It seemed the perfect setting for their little Christmas break getaway. The truth of it was, though, it didn't matter where they were. They were enveloped in the aura that comes with true friendship. The three of them continued to quench their thirst with Mexican culture, consisting mostly of Coronas, until early the next morning.

"Hey, let's go down to the beach," Hope suggested at 2:30 A.M., convincing the guys it would be fun. Intoxicated with friendship and alcohol, they half strolled, half staggered their way down to the nearby coast. They all removed their shoes and ran onto the sandy beach, soft and cold beneath their feet. The small crescent moon glistened off the white caps gently pounding the shoreline, and illuminated the beach. It was an incredible night; there were more stars out than any of them had ever seen. They sat down at the edge where the ocean rolls up to meet the beach. The tide was going out, but every now and again a wave would sneak up and caress the bottom of their feet. The water was cold, but they didn't care. They were in their own little paradise and nothing else mattered.

"Isn't it just beautiful?" Hope said. "The stars seem to go on forever and ever."

They sat back and stared up into the sky, the whole universe right next to them, as though you could reach up and grab some of the stars. Yet at the same time it felt so out of reach, far removed and unreal. They sat quietly, enjoying the silence, getting lost in the night sky. Although they were just minutes from the noise and commotion of late night bars and clubs, they were miles away in their minds. They each, in their own way, soaked up the magic of the night.

Out of the silence, Cole spoke. "Do you ever wonder what this is all about? Life, I mean. We are here on Earth in the middle of this huge universe with all of this incredible beauty. Don't you ever think about what it all means?"

"I think you've got tequila on the brain, Cole. What the hell are you talking about?" Jake replied.

"No, I am serious," Cole snapped back. "Don't you ever think about things like that? I mean, there's got to be more to life than just going to school so that we can then get some lame job that we don't like, so we can work forty years and retire with savings that would make eating at McDonald's difficult. It happened to my grandparents…yours too, Hope. I know my parents have good jobs, and we live pretty comfortably, but are they really happy? I mean, what's the point of it all anyway?"

Surprised with how philosophical their drunken friend was getting and not knowing how to respond, both Hope and Jake just sat there taking it in.

"The stars always make me think like this. Back when we were in high school, after I'd come home from being out partying with you guys, sometimes I'd go and lie in the hammock in my backyard and just stare up at the sky. It was incredible how the trees in the yard made this perfect circle for me to look up through. It was like it was my own private little observatory. Man, I would get so lost in the stars. They are endless. They are unlimited. I'd just stare up there for hours and hours and just think about everything that was going on. My parents, school, the game coming up, you guys, college, life after college—"

"There's life after college?" Jake interrupted sarcastically and they all had a big laugh.

"There was something about those stars, just like tonight, that just mesmerized me," Cole continued in a serious tone. "I would start dreaming, although I was still awake, and all of the little problems I had going on in my life would just seem to fade away."

"Problems? What the hell kind of problems do you have?" Jake spouted. "You've got great parents, unlike mine who barely notice that I am alive. You've got a great girlfriend. You are good at frickin' everything, and you don't even have to put any effort into anything. What problems could you possibly have, Cole?" he exclaimed only half believing he just said that to his best friend.

"We've all got shit to deal with, Jake. My issues are just different from yours. You know me; I am always getting into some kind of trouble. Why do you think that is? It's like I'm trapped between these two worlds: one being that everyone expects me to always do great and the other being that they always expect me to fuck up. It's like when I do good at something, it feels like I'm buying into all the bullshit I don't believe in, you know, conforming to the authority I rarely think is right. Although when I don't, I feel like I am letting myself down. I don't really know how to explain it, but it's like this incredible pressure to fit into all these places that I don't even want to be in the first place. Ah hell, what's the difference anyway? I guess it doesn't really matter."

"Of course it matters, baby," Hope spoke up. "It matters because when you are in that hammock and you lose yourself in the stars, that's the *you* I have fallen in love with. That's the *you* you are becoming. Someone who can rise above all of this crap."

"I don't know, Hopes. It just doesn't seem to fit in the 'real world.' I mean, it's great for 3 A.M. in the hammock or lying on the beach in Cabo with your friends, but it doesn't do much good when you've got to go get a job to support yourself."

"That's when it matters the most, Cole, don't you see?" Hope argued. And those were the last words that were said that night.

Hope had a way of looking at things that showed wisdom well beyond her years. Perhaps it was because she grew up with a philosophy professor for a father. Maybe it was that her mother died when she was young and she had to be strong enough to get through a lot of things on her own. Or maybe it was because Cole had so much energy going in so many different directions, that she learned how to refocus him back on track. Regardless of the reason or reasons, she and Cole shared a mutual respect. All three did. They always had.

They lay there on the beach deep in thought, thinking about everything and nothing at the same time. Jake's thoughts drifted off to when they were younger, before any of these conversations would have taken place. He thought about how free they were growing up, without responsibilities or commitments, when it was "cool" to have your parents not really care about you, and when the worst thing that happened to you was that you didn't get dessert after dinner. Things were simpler then. In a lot of ways he missed those times. And as he stared up at the stars, he knew those days would never be here again.

Hours later they awoke, still on the beach and ridiculously hung over. "I've got sand in my ass," mumbled Jake as if the others actually would care, "and in my ears, and nose.... This sucks!"

"Shhhssssssh, buddy, not so loud. A little respect for those that are hanging hard this morning," requested Cole.

"How are you feeling, honey?" Cole asked Hope, not looking in her direction.

"I'm doing fine, sweetie pie." Jake said with a chuckle. "Where the hell is Hope?"

Cole turned to where she had been lying, but she was gone. "Good morning, boys," echoed from the distance. It was Hope walking back toward the beach carrying a tray with three large coffees. "Anyone interested in some morning java?"

"If you don't marry this woman, I'm going to," Jake said, eternally grateful for his morning wake-up call.

"Hopes, did I ever tell you how much I love you?" Cole asked half jokingly.

"How much, baby?" replied Hope.

"Well, at least this much," Cole answered holding out his arms as wide as he could, then moving forward and giving Hope a big hug.

The three of them sat down to drink their coffee as the sun slowly rose in the sky behind them. "Hey, I was thinking," began Hope. "Anyone interested in driving back to campus early? If we leave today, we'll get back in time to spend a night with Pete before we have to go back home for Christmas. I figure he's probably stir-crazy and could use the company and besides, I have to do late registration for this semester."

"Sounds like a plan to me. I think everyone at State does late registration. Jake, you in?"

"Yeah, man. Let's grab some breakfast at that little place on the beach we saw coming in, then head back up the coast." Jake replied.

So they headed out for the two-day drive back to the campus and a night out with Pete. They told him about Cabo, the beers, and the tequila. But for whatever reason, no one brought up the conversation they had on the beach. They all drove back home for Christmas the next day.

But for Hope, Cole, and Jake the Cabo trip hadn't been just another party-filled weekend. They had stirred up something inside themselves while looking into the stars that night. Something that was going to continue to resurface, something they couldn't ignore, something that would change their lives forever.

CHAPTER THREE

"...We wish you a merry Christmas, we wish you a merry Christmas, we wish you a merry Christmas, and a happy New Year," echoed the carolers outside the Andersons' front door. Cole and his parents clapped and his mom gave each young caroler a dollar, which seemed to light up their faces with a joy that can't be matched any other time of year.

A white Christmas it wasn't—it rarely is in San Moreno County—but it was a joyous one all the same. The small community in which they grew up made the most of the holiday season. They did everything but bring in the snow, which they probably would have if they found a way to do it. Almost every house was decorated in lights, and every street was full of different Christmas displays celebrating the spirit of the season.

Christmas at the Andersons' was usually a festive occasion. For the last two years, Cole's family had joined together with Hope and her father, which seemed to work pretty well for everyone. On Christmas Eve there was always a big dinner. And after the morning blitzkrieg on presents, there was a huge brunch. One thing about Cole's mom, Lucy, was that she was an incredible cook. After a semester at college of eating fish tacos, macaroni and cheese, and pizza, Cole was looking forward to his mom's holiday creations.

"Cole, can you come in here a minute?" his mom called from the kitchen.

"Whatcha need, Ma?" Cole said as he walked over to her.

"Can you give me a hand with this roast? It's pretty heavy."

"Sure, no problem," he replied and lifted the roast out of the oven. Cole had never seen a bigger slab of meat. "It looks like something straight out of *The Flintstones*," he thought to himself, "a brontosaurus leg or mastodon thigh, no doubt!"

"So how is school going?" Cole's mom asked.

"Not bad, a bit boring, but my grades are pretty good. The 'gang' is all still intact, so that's making it fun. The Cabo trip was a great time. We're thinking about doing it again, maybe in the summer. It was really good to unwind after finals, before having to go back and do it all over again," Cole said.

He had always been able to talk with his parents. Although they didn't always see eye to eye on things and would put their foot down if they disagreed, they were generally open to hearing his thoughts. It was something he often took for granted growing up. But as he began to see the kind of relationship Jake had with his parents, Cole started to appreciate his own parents more and more.

Cole probably inherited his emotional side from his mom. She was a wonderful woman with a huge heart. She could lift the anyone's spirits with her warm eyes and great big smile, and had a knack for always looking at the brighter side of things. She was the kind of mom who loved to make kids happy. She would invite Cole's friends over to join them for dinner or just to hang out, whenever possible.

If his mom was the emotional glue in the family, his dad, Ben, was the doer. As a corporate executive with a large telecommunications company in Los Angeles, Ben Anderson traveled often and also commuted to and from work. Still he managed to make time for Cole, especially when it came to athletics. His father had coached and encouraged him as he grew up and they generally got along. Cole, however, often felt his dad pushed him too hard.

All in all, they had become a pretty happy family, but it certainly hadn't always been that way. In the early years of high school, as Cole was just starting to develop his own views about the way he wanted to live, they often had knock-down, drag-out battles about either his long hair, or his messy clothes, or his wrong attitude. You name it; they fought about it. As time passed, things settled down. Whether Cole started growing up and changing, or his parents started to see things more his way, the result was that they had a much better relationship.

"How come Peter didn't go with you?" his mom asked.

"He had to be at baseball practice. It started early. We told him we would toast a beer to him…ah…a…I mean a Coke to him." Cole quickly remembered who he was talking to and that he was only nineteen. The truth was, his parents treated him as an adult, and as long as he was being responsible, they didn't care much if he had a few beers.

"Yeah, yeah, I know…a Coke. Really. Like I believe that, Cole. Well, you made it back in one piece and you didn't wreck the Jeep, so it couldn't have been too bad," his mom said laughing.

"Can you pass the potatoes please, Mr. Anderson?" Hope asked as they sat down to dinner.

"Here you go, Hope," replied Cole's father. "So, Cole tells me you had a good trip to Mexico last week."

"Yes, we really did. It was a lot of fun. None of us had ever been to Cabo before, so we took our time getting down there, you know, seeing the coast and everything, and hung out on the beach for a bit. It was really beautiful there. And cheap too," she added. "Dad, you told me you've been there before, right?"

"Oh, you have, Clayton? When did you go?" asked Lucy.

"Yes, I have indeed. It was when I was back in college as well. I went to school at UC at Berkeley, and one year a bunch of us went on this incredible road trip during summer break. What a tremendous experience that was. In many ways, Hope, it was a lot like the trip you guys had. It was my first real getaway, so to speak, without my parents. I learned a lot during that little excursion. I learned how to get by without much money, what true friends really were, and most importantly, a lot about myself. Unfortunately, I learned a little too much about beer and tequila," laughed Mr. Stewart.

They all had a good laugh, including Ben and Lucy. They had been a little nervous about letting Cole go in the first place, but they had decided to trust Cole to at least stay out of major trouble.

They talked, laughed, and enjoyed each other's company. There was something different about this evening. There weren't any family quarrels or major arguments. It was fairly odd. Generally when they all got together, something would come up to cause a little scuffle. But not this year; something had changed. It was as though the parents were looking at the kids differently. Perhaps now that they were off to college they saw them as adults and were treating them that way. Or maybe it was Cole and Hope who were changing, gaining a little maturity, growing up a bit. Or maybe the adults were just in better moods because now that the kids were out of the house, they had more time to themselves. Whatever it was, both Cole and Hope could feel it. They never talked about it, but they both knew. Whatever it was that had changed, they liked it.

As dinner was breaking up, Cole noticed something out of the corner of his eye. There was a hint of smoke coming from the backyard. At first he was alarmed, but he soon realized what it was. He motioned for Hope to join him and they went out to investigate. They found Jake lying in the hammock, smoking a joint. It was clear he was upset. His face was a little red and it looked as if he may have been crying.

"I remembered what you said about this hammock when we were in Cabo," began Jake, "and how the stars helped you to forget all of the problems you had in life, so I decided to give it a try. I've actually been out here for about two hours, watching you all talk and laugh. All of you looked so nice in there. It's really great to see a family having fun together, getting along, and enjoying each other's company."

Jake came from a family where loving each other wasn't a high priority. His parents had married young and, although that isn't always a recipe for disaster, in this case it was. For years, Jake's parents treated him almost as if he wasn't their child. It was a disturbing situation Hope and Cole knew all too well. During high school, every few months Jake would have to "get away" for a few days while things settled down and would end up staying with either Cole or Pete.

There may have been a lot of things either Cole or Hope could say to make Jake feel better but, for some reason, they sat on the grass next to their friend and just listened to him. They sensed he only needed someone to talk to. Often that's the best kind of friend: one who knows when to just listen.

"Man, they can be such bastards sometimes. It's not like they couldn't have at least pretended to get along during the holidays when I was home or saved their shit until after I left. No, they had to pick tonight to let the stones fly. Oh, I guess I really don't care. It's been so long since I've seen them happy together. Remember how many times in high school I said I wished they'd just get a divorce, so the fighting would stop?" Jake asked, looking over at Cole and Hope. They stayed silent and nodded. "Well, they say to be careful what you ask for, because you just might get it. So Christmas Eve at the Nelsons' was celebrated with my parents telling me they are divorcing. Great sense of timing, huh? Merry fucking Christmas!

"You know, I don't even know why I'm upset, but I guess a part of me always felt like it was my fault they didn't get along. I guess in the back of my mind I wanted them to work it out and be happy. Ah Christ, Cole, where does this leave me? I'm not interested in living with either one of them. They both make me sick. They got married for all the wrong reasons. They didn't really love each other. Hell, if my mom didn't get pregnant with me, they probably never would have ended up together." Emmmphfff. Jake took another big hit. Blowing it out, he said, "What a night…hell, what a life!"

"Hey, pass that thing over here, Bogart!" Cole said motioning to the joint and trying to lighten the mood. It caused Jake to crack about a quarter of a smile, but you could tell he wasn't ready to laugh.

"So, I came over here to sit in the magic hammock to see if it would take my troubles away. You're right though, Cole. It's killer, looking up through these trees here."

"Anything you need, just ask, all right?" Cole reassured. "Why don't you stay with us until you figure some things out?"

"That's great, thanks. But let's stay out here awhile, I don't want to go in just yet, okay?"

Cole lay back and replied, "Yeah, sure man, whatever you want. Hey, you hungry? There's enough food inside to satisfy the munchies of the total student population at State."

"Naw…not right now. You know, I was thinking. Family is supposed to be there for you, and support you, and help you when you need it, and to laugh with and cry with, and all of that, right?" Jake asked.

They both just looked on and nodded. "Well, you two and Pete have been the only real family I've ever had. You're the only ones I've ever been able to count on. So, with all that's happened, I really just wanted to say 'thanks.'"

"There's no need to thank us," Hope said. "That's what friends do for each other. You've always got a family as long as you have us."

"Yeah, Jake, you know we'll always be here for you. Man, I can think of more than one instance when you've saved me from a world of hurt. Remember that time when we were in eighth grade and we Saran-wrapped that kid to the flagpole?" Cole said laughing.

"What?" Hope said. "You did what? I didn't really know you guys back then."

"Oh yeah, it was great. We were in eighth grade and it was back when we thought it was cool to pick on the nerdy kids. God, we were little terrors back then. I honestly don't know how anyone put up with us. We were always getting into some kind of trouble. So one day, there was a fire drill and we were all outside in front of the school waiting for the bell to ring so we could go back in. Do you remember how the teachers always used to make a big deal about coming back in right away, and how they didn't want anyone hanging around in the parking lot?" Cole said.

Hope nodded her head yes.

"Well, we took this kid—hell I can't even remember his name—and we Saran-wrapped him from head to toe to the flag pole. From far away, it looked like he was just leaning against the pole 'cause you couldn't see the clear wrap that held him there unless you were up close. So, the teachers were all calling to him to come in and it looked like he was just standing there, totally ignoring them. They were yelling at him and couldn't understand why he just stood there, without even answering them. We had covered up his mouth too and just left his nose open. He could breath, but he couldn't say a word. God, was it hilarious!

"Anyway," Cole continued, "so the teachers finally went out there and cut him down, and when they asked him who had done this to him, he didn't tell them. Who knows why, but he didn't. Somehow, the principal heard the rumor that I was the one who did it, and she called me down to her office. She had me in there giving me the third degree, and I kept denying it and telling her that I had nothing to do with it. Since she didn't have any proof, she couldn't really do anything. While we were in her office, she had the kid—oh yeah, Tim. Yeah, his name was Tim. Anyway, Tim was waiting outside her office to talk to her next."

"Pete and I grabbed him," Jake interrupted, "and wrapped him up again in Saran wrap and leaned him against the principal's door. Oh, it was so classic, Hope. We knocked on the door and ran. When she opened her door, li'l ole Tim came falling in, head first."

"I laughed so hard I almost pissed in my pants," Cole jumped back in. "Yeah, and because she knew I wasn't involved that time, she figured I didn't do it the first time and she let me off. None of us ever got caught for that one. Man, was that a riot. Too damn funny."

They all broke into hysterical laughter and for a brief moment forgot about Jake's situation. Although the moment came and went, they had the release they needed. Jake's thoughts were no longer dominated by his problems at home. In a unique way, the magic hammock worked. Just as it had helped release Cole from his life problems, it had done the same for Jake.

"Hey, I betcha they have the apple pie and stuff out by now. Who's up for dessert?" Cole asked.

"For apple pie, I guess I could be convinced to go in. Let's go," Jake said, feeling a little bit more like himself for the first time that night.

"Hey, let's call Pete," Hope suddenly added. "He's got to go back to school the day after tomorrow."

"You've got to love this woman," remarked Cole to Jake, agreeing with her.

They went inside and Pete showed up a few minutes later. The four of them sat around with Cole's parents and Hope's dad talking about school, sports, and plans after college. And although nobody really had any, they each had various theories as to why they still had plenty of time to figure it all out. They did have a great many laughs that night. They had a great Christmas. They had great friends.

CHAPTER FOUR

The three arrived back at school a few days before classes started. After dropping Hope off, Jake and Cole went over to their house to see what Pete was up to. As they pulled open the front door, they were greeted by a loud shriek.

"Ahhhhhhhhhhhh!" screamed a girl, standing naked with her hand on the refrigerator door.

"Well, I guess Pete's home," Jake said, laughing while he enjoyed the view.

"Good afternoon, young lady," Cole said sarcastically. The girl, whom neither of them had ever seen before, was considerably embarrassed and quickly moved behind the refrigerator door to conceal herself from their view. "Are you our welcome-home present?"

"Very funny, but no. Do you think you guys can close your eyes so I can go to the bedroom and get dressed?" asked the naked stranger.

"Well, Jake my friend, this is what you would call a 'compromising situation,'" Cole started in, speaking in a very dignified voice. He could sense the girl was a good sport, so he wasn't worried about pushing it too far.

Besides, he loved to push things too far. "As I see it, if she was comfortable enough to walk from the bedroom to the kitchen, she should be just as comfortable to walk back, right?" Cole declared as if his statement were perfectly logical.

"Hey, I don't know about that," she called out. "Peter!"

"Wait a minute, you look r-r-really familiar." In the presence of a naked beauty, Jake was a bit nervous. "This sounds bad, but I am pretty s-s-sure we have met before. Holy shit!" Jake shouted, as his memory clicked in, "you're the 'ass in your face' g-g-girl from the ta-taco stand."

She just smiled and remained crouched behind the refrigerator door.

"Happy New Year, guys!" Pete wandered into the kitchen from the back room, tossing a towel to his house guest. She wrapped herself up and quickly walked into the back to get dressed.

"That's the girl from the taco place, before break, right?" Jake asked, but knew it was.

"One and the same. We ran into each other again last week and have hung out a bit since. She's fantastic…I think she could be 'the one.'"

Jake looked at Cole and they both burst out laughing. Since they were sixteen, almost every girl that Pete even kissed was "the one," for at least a few minutes. Although Pete had no trouble meeting women, he got emotionally involved quickly and often, and his relationships had all been about the same. He met someone, they got serious, he fell in love, and then it ended as fast as it had begun. He was perpetually stuck in romance and his relationships were fast, furious, then finished.

"I don't think you can call it 'the one' anymore, Pete. I think by now, you're on about 'the tenth,'" bellowed Jake, breaking into laughter.

"Hey, if you say she's the one, I believe you," said Cole with a straight face. Jake looked puzzled by his friend's willingness to let this opportunity to poke fun at Pete go by.

"Thanks for the faith, man. I appreciate that," Pete said

"So what's her name?" Cole asked still with a straight face.

"Debra," Pete said proudly.

"And her last name?" said Cole, smirking.

"Last name? A…um…ah, shiiiit…you guys suck!" Pete turned and stormed out of the room as Jake and Cole fell onto the couch laughing uncontrollably.

The next day Hope, Pete, Cole, and Jake were sitting at an outdoor deck having lunch talking about the upcoming semester. They all concluded the campus was designed by an extremely intelligent individual who understood the necessity of having a café with an outdoor beer garden right in the middle of everything. Since the entire gang had bought fake IDs from one of the more enterprising students on campus earlier in the semester, they made it a point to put them to good use. The café was a small establishment called The Tavern, which they frequented often. With the pristine weather of San Diego County, and more than thirty thousand thirsty college students, an outdoor table at The Tavern was a hard-to-come-by commodity.

"Other than the basics we all have, what classes did you guys take?" Hope inquired.

Jake was the first to respond. "I'm taking a basic psychology class."

"I am taking family planning," Pete replied next.

"Isn't that class really for women?" Hope shot back, beating Jake and Cole to the obvious question.

"Exactly!" Pete exclaimed, nodding his head and smiling.

"What about the 'ass girl'—Debra?" Jake chimed in.

"Oh well, just in case, you know. I don't want to close off my options just yet." They all had a laugh in Pete's honor.

"What about you, Cole? What are you taking?" inquired Hope.

"I'm taking that 'mind, body, spirit' class with Professor McIntry," Cole responded.

"So you decided to take it after all. It's the first class we'll have together. That's great, Cole," said Hope, excited about his decision.

"Man, I heard that McIntry guy was a nutball," said Pete.

"Yeah, he's almost been kicked out of here, like four times. I heard his class is pretty weird too," echoed Jake.

"What's weird, anyway?" Cole replied. "I'm weird. Pete's weird. Well, Hope's pretty normal. But, Jake, you're as weird as they come. So what. It actually looks like an interesting class and I don't think I've ever said that before. Hell, I might even learn something useful. What a concept that would be!

"I heard a lot about Professor McIntry, too," Cole continued. "I heard about him before we even got down here. Supposedly he's a good teacher but a little 'out there.'

I met this girl during last semester who had him about a year ago. She said the class was incredible. She said it taught her so much about herself, about the world, and all kinds of things in metaphysical studies. I guess Professor McIntry uses some pretty cutting-edge ways of teaching. Some of the other teachers—and even some of the parents—have tried to get him fired for teaching material that is too advanced. Some say it's sacrilegious, but he's had as many supporters as critics. I just think a lot of people don't understand him."

"The poor misunderstood professor. That's what they say about all the weird people," Pete scoffed.

"Yeah, like Einstein, and da Vinci, and Martin Luther. All those kinds of weird people, Pete?" Cole replied quickly.

"Great thinkers have often been misunderstood during their own lifetime," Hope began. "It's usually not until years later that people really understand their brilliance. Think about how many people thought Einstein was absolutely bonkers. Even today, anyone who dares to 'rock the boat,' so to speak, usually gets labeled as being insane or anti- this or that. It's sad, when you think about it. It doesn't give someone much incentive to be creative, or different, or really put themselves out there. I think it's changing though and getting a little better. I think people are starting to realize 'the average way' isn't working so well. So different—or as you say, Pete, 'weird'—isn't so bad."

Hope was passionate about civil liberties, such as freedom of speech and self-expression. She had been around free and creative thinking all her life. Growing up mostly with her father—who went back to his alma mater, UC Berkeley, to teach philosophy—she was exposed to many of the great thinkers throughout history, such as Emerson, Pythagoras, Thoreau, and Marcus Aurelius. Everyone always thought she would end up being a lawyer or a politician, one of the good ones, that is. But Hope hadn't figured it out yet.

Perhaps that was why she loved Cole so much. Most people thought they were very different, because externally they really appeared different. Many people who thought they knew what was "best" for Hope didn't understand what she saw in him. Cole was a charismatic character. He was good looking but didn't seem to have much depth. Hope knew the truth. She knew the Cole "behind the Cole" who was trying so hard to break free. Cole knew it too and had opened up to her many times. That night in Cabo, however, was the first time he had ever talked like that around Jake. Cole had an uneasiness about the future. Although he felt he was changing inside, he didn't know how to let go of all the things that held him back.

"Well, all right. Enough of that!" Pete exclaimed. "It's Saturday and class doesn't start until Monday, so I don't want to hear anything that requires me to think for the rest of the weekend! Is that a deal?"

"Deal!" Hope, Cole, and Jake all said at the same time. Pete had a way of always bringing things down to a basic level. A philosopher he wasn't, but he was a great friend and they all knew it.

"Hopes, how about just you and me tonight?" Cole whispered, smiling.

"That would be great. What time?" Hope replied.

"I'll come get ya at around eight."

"Oh, the little love birds. See you at eight, honey bunny…smoochy, smoochy," Jake mocked. Then, looking at Pete, "Petey, how about just you and me tonight, big fella?"

Pete jokingly put his arm around Jake and they started skipping away, as Cole and Hope laughed.

"Hey, wait up guys!" Cole shouted. "I'll see you at eight, baby. Love ya!" Cole shouted back to Hope and ran to catch up. Without missing a beat, he threw his arm about Jake and started skipping along with them. If you didn't know them, you would have thought they were crazy. Sometimes in life though, you need to get a little crazy with your friends. Hope looked on, thinking, "What a bunch of kooks. I just love them all."

CHAPTER FIVE

"What a great spot," Hope said as Cole laid out the blanket. They had driven up to a little hilltop in Point Loma, a small quaint city in San Diego County, and found a nice clearing to sit down in. It was a beautiful clear night. Cole had packed a picnic basket with red wine, grapes, and brie, picked up Hope, and bought two cracked lobsters. A romantic deep down inside, Cole wanted to make the last night of break really special for Hope. Fortunately, Cole's mom was a romantic too. When he told her what he wanted to do, she graciously gave him some money to finance his hilltop date. Cole's mom liked Hope—it was hard not to—and she knew Hope was good for Cole. When they were together, Cole's mom didn't worry about their getting into trouble. She felt comfortable Hope would probably talk Cole out of any crazy idea he might come up with.

As Cole started to discover more and more about himself, he thought a lot about his relationship with Hope. Why wasn't he faithful? What did that say about him? He had a fantastic woman who completely adored him, as he did her. Yet he still found himself searching. Why?

As Pete would say, it was the thrill of the game that kept the fires burning. It was the chase not the conquest that interested them. But recently, Cole started to understand how much his relationship with Hope actually meant to him. If he lost her, what would he do then? How much would the chase actually fulfill him, without knowing he had Hope to come back to? Recent events—like being home over the holidays, Jake's parents getting divorced, and Christmas break in Cabo—had taught him the value of finding someone like Hope, who you could share your heart with. He started seeing for the first time how much Hope had actually helped him grow, and he started falling in love with her all over again. It was time more than just one person put effort into their relationship.

"Good evening, *madame*, welcome to *Le Café de Cole*. Please have a seat while we get your dinner ready," Cole said in his best French accent. Hope loved it. She sat back and watched and fell more in love with each word he spoke.

"Would ze young lady care for a glass of wine?" he continued.

"That would be perfect, thank you," she said, loving the effort he was putting in.

He poured two glasses. "For tonight's selection, we have a wonderful dinner prepared, guaranteed to dance on ze palate and entertain ze taste buds. First, we start off with some cheese and fruit," he said placing them on the blanket. "Would ze lady do me ze honor of allowing me to feed her?"

Hope smiled broadly and nodded. She lay there like a queen as Cole fed her a grape. Before he could give her a second, she pulled him close and planted a big kiss on her French waiter.

"Wow!" exclaimed Cole. "And we haven't even gotten to the lobster yet. This is gonna be a great night."

"It already is," Hope said, feeling absolutely wonderful.

And it was a great night. They sat on the hill overlooking San Diego and shared wine, fruit, lobster, and themselves under the stars. It was nice to have time for just the two of them. It was rare they got the chance to get away like this without school, or family, or Pete and Jake. They lay there, looking up, indulging themselves in one of Cole's favorite things—staring up at the neverending sky and looking deep into the wisdom of the universe.

"I am pretty excited about this class with Professor McIntry," Cole said without taking his eyes off the sky.

"Me too, it should be an incredible experience. He is definitely the most progressive teacher I have ever heard of," shared Hope.

"I've just got so much going on inside my head right now, Hope. I mean, I've always had a lot going on, but some of the things are actually starting to make sense. I've always had so much chaos inside that I never seemed to know which end was up. But it's almost like I've had this sense that there has to be something more, and not just more of the same, but a different way of doing things, a different way of looking at things. I don't know, honey, but I feel like something is starting to happen. It may sound crazy, but it's like there's this other person inside of me that I've been holding back all of this time, and it's kicking and screaming like hell to get out. Is that crazy, or what?" Cole said.

"Not at all, baby, not at all," Hope replied.

"Jake probably thought I was losing my mind when I said all that stuff in Mexico, huh?" Cole asked.

"You'd be surprised. I think Jake probably related to it more than you think. After all, he went straight for the 'magic hammock,' as he called it," Hope said.

"Yeah, I guess. You know, Jake's parents splitting up really made me think about my family."

"I know what you mean. I thought a lot about my mom. You know, I was only six when she died," remembered Hope. "I started thinking how much her death changed our family, how much it changed my dad and me."

"Yeah, everything changes, that's for sure. Do you miss your mom, Hopes?"

"Well, I don't remember her, as a person, enough to really miss her. But I think I miss having a mom," Hope answered. "Dad's done a great job raising me—"

"Oh, come on, Hope, both of us know you are the one raising him," Cole said quickly.

"Yeah, I guess that's more or less true," Hope responded. "It makes you just think about how important family really is."

"Exactly. If you remember when we first met, when we were around fourteen or fifteen—"

"June 2, 1995. We were fifteen," Hope interrupted as they both chuckled at her knowing the exact date.

"Well, if you remember, I didn't get along that well with my parents back then. We were always fighting and arguing. You know how they were either harassing me about my hair, or the music I listened to, or my 'shitty attitude'…all that kind of stuff," Cole stated.

Hope just nodded in understanding.

"Well, I was thinking about when things started to get better. It was around the time I was graduating and getting ready to leave for school. You know, that's when I started changing. It was almost like I expected to have to fight with my parents about stuff, so that's exactly what happened. I mean, I'm not saying it was all my fault, 'cause there certainly were times when they were just being stupid. But looking back, I understand a lot more about where they were coming from.

"It's like I was fighting so hard to be different, to be an individual and make my own choices that sometimes I did things just because I knew it would piss them off, or piss anybody off, like a coach or a teacher, or some crap like that. God, I must have put them through hell. 'Cause as you know, baby, I can be a downright bastard sometimes," Cole concluded.

"You know, I never really noticed." Hope replied sarcastically.

"Yeah, right," Cole said and they both laughed. "Well, anyway, Jake's problem just made me think." He paused, then added, "Wonder what Jake and Pete are up to right now."

"Probably no good, I would guess. It's the last weekend before school starts. I am sure they're combing the bars, half drunk. Pete probably already has a half-a-dozen phone numbers—"

"Yeah, and Jake has stuttered his way out of two or three," Cole interrupted. They both knew it wasn't really funny but, ever since they could remember, Jake had a stuttering problem around women. By this point it had grown into a standing joke. The guy could give a speech in front of a hundred people and not miss a beat. But you get him in front of a woman in a tight shirt and he couldn't get ten words out without hitting a speed bump.

"So yeah, I'm the starting shortstop for varsity baseball," Pete said to an attractive little brunette he had struck up a conversation with at the bar. The fact that Coach Numbnuts hadn't named the starters yet seemed insignificant to Pete at the moment. "I figure if I do well this year, I'll have a good shot at all-American next year…hell, maybe even this year. I've gotten a few calls from the Yankees and the White Sox, saying they're gonna be watching my college career."

"That's great. So you're going to play in the pros?" asked the girl, impressed with Pete's baseball prowess.

"I'm really not sure just yet, I want to leave my options open," Pete responded as if he didn't care either way. The truth wasn't the most important thing with Pete when it came to talking to ladies. The funny thing was, he didn't see it as lying. Most of the stories he came up with were so farfetched, he figured it was their fault if they bought into them. It was a fairly warped perspective; but then again, Pete was fairly warped.

Pete knew he could hook up with this girl if he wanted to, but for some reason he just lost interest. He lost interest in being at the bar altogether. He said a quick "goodbye" to the girl he was talking with, but not before she could stuff her phone number into his front pants pocket. Then he made his way over to Jake.

"Hey, I'm gonna head home, Jake. Do you want to come with, or are you gonna stay?" asked Pete.

"Naw, I'm gonna hang out for a bit. I'll catcha later," Jake replied, and Pete turned to leave.

"So what di-di-did you sa-sa-say your name was?" Jake said, finally getting the whole question out to the girl he had started a conversation with at the bar.

"It's Susan and I already knows yours is Jake," she replied. "Am I making you nervous?"

"Wh-wh-why do you sa-say that?" Jake asked, having to laugh at himself even before he could get out the last of his sentence.

"Don't think I'm rude for asking, but have you always had that stutter?" Susan asked delicately.

"Well, actually I only have the pro-problem when I'm around go-go-good–looking women," Jake stammered.

She liked that he could laugh at himself. And she liked his honesty and candor in a time when far too many guys were like Pete. Though usually well intentioned, most guys lacked the substance she found interesting. They were so focused on impressing a girl, they rarely let down their guards long enough to get to know her. Jake was different though. He was genuine. He was real—stutter and all. With Jake, what you saw was what you got.

"Then I guess I should be flattered," Susan replied. "Can I buy you a drink?"

If there was ever a time in Jake's life when he fell for a girl in an instant, it was now. This girl was almost too good to be true. First she was flattered by his stutter; now she was buying him a drink. In that moment, Jake had a tremendous feeling of appreciation for life. It's moments like this that are a reminder of how incredible the human spirit can be. As the bartender poured his beer, Jake knew his life would be okay. Bad parents and all, he knew things would work out. He thought to himself how simple things actually were. Even with all the tragedy and chaos that had gone on in his life recently, the smallest gesture from a more-or-less complete stranger could make all his troubles fade away. Time seemed to stop completely. It was as if his entire life was inside that fifteen seconds. He looked around and saw everything moving in slow motion. It seemed to last forever. He wanted it to last forever. What an absolute sense of freedom he felt. What an incredible sense of gratitude he had for this stranger, Susan, who had been the catalyst.

"Thank you," Jake said boldly. "Thank you very much."

"It's just a beer," Susan responded hearing the way Jake thanked her like she had just saved his life.

"Actually, it's not just a beer. I mean-i-i-it's not just the beer. I r-r-really appreciate it," Jake said, realizing how funny it must sound to her. She hadn't had the incredible dream that he did just a second ago. She didn't experience time standing still while the beer was being poured. She didn't just have her life touched by a stranger. She couldn't possibly understand.

Although this amount of gratitude was a bit weird for a beer, Susan was overwhelmed by Jake's emotion. Still, she didn't know what to think. He appeared to be a student, but perhaps he was homeless and didn't have any money. Maybe he was an alcoholic and this beer meant everything to him. Or maybe he was just a sincere guy who had been going through some tough times. All of these absurd thoughts went through her head at the same time. She still thought he was a little strange but, nevertheless, she was touched.

"So what are you studying, Jake?" Susan asked, knowing she needed to change the subject.

"Ah—it's just m-m-my second semester, so I'm still taking th-th-the basics. I haven't really decided what I'm g-going to major in y-y-yet. Probably j-just liberal arts," Jake finally got out. "What about you?"

"This is my third year. I'm a psychology major. I'm not sure what I am going to do with it yet, but I want to stay in some sort of human relations or service-oriented field," Susan replied.

"Hey, a psych major? My friends and I were talking about this c-c-class they are taking this semester. It's taught by this p-p-professor who people say is a bit off the wall. I wonder if you've taken it?" Jake said, remembering his earlier conversation with Cole and Hope.

"You can only be talking about Professor McIntry's class, 'mind, body, spirit,'" Susan said knowingly.

"Yeah, how did you know?" Jake asked curiously.

"The professor and his class have quite a reputation. People are either afraid of it or love it. But everyone knows about it. Yeah, I took it last year. It was the best class I have ever taken. It's more than just a class though; it changed my life," Susan said, getting excited as she talked about it. "I still meet once a month with some ex-students from that class. We have a study group about the things we learned there."

"You're kidding. You go to a study g-g-group for a class you haven't had for a year? Why?" Jake asked, puzzled.

"Like I said, it's more than just a class—it's really hard to explain. It's one of those things that really only makes sense to you when you have experienced it. Kind of like what just happened to you when I bought that beer for you. Obviously something was going on inside of you that had very little to do with what was actually going on here in the bar. It wouldn't be easy to explain, would it?" Susan paused then added, "All I can say is that your friends are in for an incredible journey."

Jake was taken by her perceptiveness. And she had piqued his curiosity about the infamous professor's class. He decided to see about picking it up last minute, if there was any space left in the class. "Hey, Susan, it's getting late and I am g-go-going to run, but would you like to get together s-s-sometime?" Jake asked.

"I'd really like that, Jake," Susan remarked. "Here's my number. Give me a call when you want to get together."

"I will. Hey, and—ah—thanks again for the beer," he said, knowing she would understand the double meaning of his statement. He did his best to stay composed while he was still in front of her at the bar. The truth, though, was that he felt so alive he could hardly contain himself. He had met someone without having to tell some outrageous story, like Pete usually did. And she had genuine interest in him, stutter and all. He walked home with an incredible sense of joy. Joy about meeting Susan, about life and about himself. For the first time in a long while, Jake had met someone he could really see himself with. She took him for what he was, and he liked that. He liked that a lot.

CHAPTER SIX

"My God, I don't think that I've ever been nervous walking into a class for the first time before," Cole said to Jake and Hope as they approached the lecture hall where Professor McIntry's class was held.

"That's because you've never taken any of them seriously before, Cole," Hope commented.

"Yeah, and you usually never made it to the first day either," Jake added jokingly. "Man, I hope I can get into this class—" He stopped in mid-sentence when he noticed the huge crowd of students outside the hall. "I guess I'm not the only one hoping to register last minute. Look at this frickin' line."

"Everyone inside, please," the professor bellowed from within the lecture hall. The entire crowd wedged itself into the auditorium. There were seats for about two hundred people and they were all full. There were another eighty or ninety people standing on the sides and in the back of the room. "Is everyone in?" he asked.

"Yes, sir," someone shouted from the back.

"Please close the door," Professor McIntry said, then he turned off the lights. "I want you all to close your eyes.

Yes, close your eyes and keep them closed." A few laughs and giggles were heard through the crowd. Then as it got silent he continued, "Relax. Get comfortable whether sitting or standing. Once you're comfortable, I want you to visualize an apple on the picture screen of your mind. Let your imagination create the image. Can you see it? It's a brilliant shade of red. It has a stem with a small green leaf on the top. It's just been washed, so it has a few drops of water resting gently on top. It looks like it will taste so juicy and delicious that your mouth actually is starting to salivate. Can you feel the saliva start to build up in your mouth? Concentrate on the feeling of what that apple tastes like. Bite into it. Feel the juice of the apple on your tongue and cheeks. It's delicious. Fully experience the taste." He took a long pause, probably twenty seconds or so, then said, "Now open your eyes."

"Okay," the professor continued, "we'll come back to that in a minute. There are 215 spots in this class and there are far more people here than that. I am sure that many of you are here for no other reason than to see for yourself if I actually am as psychotic as you have heard I am." The class interrupted him with some guilty laughter. "I want you to understand right now that whatever you have heard about me is but a fraction of how unglued from everyday reality I really am. And I would venture to guess many of you are here because you heard we don't use any textbook for this class, so it won't cost you any extra money. Oh, but don't be fooled by the overly obvious. There is a cost to everything in life, my young little journeymen. Indeed, there is. Together we shall create our own textbook throughout the semester, which is certainly a much more difficult task.

"We have only two rules in this class, and these rules apply to me as much as they do to you. The first is complete honesty on all matters, regardless of how emotionally difficult something may seem. Second, complete and willing participation. Do we understand?" he asked.

"Yes," the audience answered together.

"Wonderful. Now, it's clear many of you who are here right now will not fit into this class. Some of you who are registered may decide to drop and others may join us. There are only seventeen spots open as of right now, with about sixty or seventy people interested in getting in. So, what shall we do?

"Is there anyone who has already changed their mind and doesn't want to take the class?" the professor asked. Surprisingly, five people got up and left. "Okay, now we're getting somewhere. How many people did not close their eyes during that stupid little experiment we did a minute ago with the apple? Remember rule number one: complete honesty." About forty or so people raised their hands.

"Wonderful," he continued. "Thank you for your honesty. It probably wasn't easy to admit that in front of everyone, was it? Let this be an example for the rest of the class to learn from," he said. "Okay, those who have their hands up, please leave. You are dismissed. Feel free to register next semester if you like. Remember rule number two: complete and willing participation. Is that correct?"

"Yes," said the remaining students, some of whom were laughing.

"Okay then. Please, exit quietly. Any of you who were actually preregistered, come see me after class and I will sign your drop slip. Only those who are willing to learn can be taught. You may have heard the saying, 'When the student is ready, the teacher will appear.' My suggestion to those who are leaving now is always be ready to learn life's lessons. Indeed, you have learned a valuable one today. Thank you for your interest in the class. Perhaps our paths will cross again in the future.

"All right, my fellow journeymen. Those who are left, can you please fill any empty seats? Thank you." The students quickly scattered to find seats, and when they had, there was no one left standing.

"Well, it looks like we have our class for this semester," the professor stated. "I love how life always shows us exactly what to do when we pay attention. Anyone who isn't registered, please see me after class and I will sign your card as well. Welcome to 'mind, body, spirit.'"

There was an energy present in the lecture hall that neither Cole, Jake, nor Hope had ever felt before. It was like the feeling you get in your stomach as the roller coaster car approaches the top arc of the steepest hill on the ride. There was an incredible anticipation filled with fear, nervousness, excitement, confusion, and adrenaline—all wrapped into one. Even with all of these emotions, the classroom felt very safe. There was an unknown element present. Who was this teacher who tells fifty people to leave just for not closing their eyes? Even people who were preregistered? Was he really crazy like everyone said? The three of them sat there, looking at each other, but not daring to say a word.

Professor McIntry was a man of about forty, with brownish hair and a rough beard. He dressed as if he didn't care much about clothes, with his shirt untucked and flip-flops for shoes. He wasn't what you would call overweight, but you might refer to him as "healthy." If you looked at his slight paunch, you could tell he was a man who didn't miss many meals. And he certainly didn't miss his opportunity to have a beer with a friend. He had an unpolished exterior. But if you viewed the professor only from the outside in, you'd miss everything that made him who he was. There was a peacefulness about him that could not be mistaken, along with an internal power and conviction that was clear to anyone who met him. He had strong but gentle green eyes—the kind of eyes that could look right through you and see directly into your soul. The kind that couldn't lie. The kind you couldn't lie to.

"How's your spirit today, class?" the professor inquired smiling brightly.

The class looked back at the professor with puzzled looks on their faces, not understanding how to respond to his question. How was their spirit? What did he mean by that?

"You all look so confused. It's not like I just asked you what the square root of 2,678 was," the professor said. Then he continued. "Is it not your spirit that you feel with? When you wipe away all the external emotions and conditions and prejudices, is it not the human spirit that you are left with? Indeed it serves us all well, my fellow journeymen, to look beneath the outer shell of humanity to find the beauty of the spirit in every person and every thing. It is in the laboratory of the spirit that greatness is conjured from the nuts and bolts of our hearts and souls," he looked at the perplexed class, paused, then said, "Don't worry. We've got all semester."

"So let's get back to the apple, shall we?" Professor McIntry said as he began to address the class again. "How many people could see the apple clearly?" He peered out over the class and saw many of them with their hands raised. "How many of you had trouble focusing on it, or seeing it at all?" About a third of the class put up their hands this time. "For those of you who could see the apple clearly, I bet your mouth salivated when I told you to bite into the apple, didn't it?" he asked.

Many in the class nodded their head "yes," but still didn't know where he was going with all of this.

"Why? Why did your mouth salivate? The apple wasn't real. It was only in your imagination, right? Why would your mouth produce saliva for an imaginary apple?" the professor asked and paused, waiting to see if anyone was bold enough to suggest the first answer of the semester.

"Nobody? Nobody even wants to guess?"

"Maybe our mind didn't know the difference," someone shouted from the back.

"Give that man a gold star," replied the professor, "that's exactly right. Your mind doesn't know the difference. Your subconscious mind, including your imagination, views everything as real. As real as you view the chairs you are sitting in right now. This is something we will spend a substantial amount of time on this semester, learning how to create your own reality.

"For those who had difficulty actually seeing the apple in your mind's eye, don't concern yourself with it just now. We will spend a lot of time this semester practicing visualization and showing you how to gain better control over your mind. Why is it important to control your thoughts, you might ask? Why is it important to make your mouth water just by imagining an apple? Surely it's more than just a game you play with yourself, right? The answer is very simple. The quality of your life is directly related to the quality of your thoughts. If you understand nothing else this semester, which unfortunately many of you may not," the professor said smiling, "understand that last statement. Since half of you probably missed it, I will say it again. The quality of your life is directly related to the quality of your thoughts.

"You see, my fellow journeymen—," he interrupted himself. "Let me stop right there. I want to make sure that all of the young ladies in our classroom understand when I say 'journeymen,' I am referring to everyone here. I am certainly not excluding the women in the class or even trying to get a rise out of those of you who consider yourselves to be feminists. Excuse my lack of political correctness for not referring to you as 'journeypeople' or 'journeypersons,' but I have never been one to be correct by political standards. So 'journeymen' you all are! Agreed?"

Half of the class said 'yes' and the other half nodded, but most of them laughed.

"So, my fellow journeymen," Professor McIntry continued, "we have a tough task to accomplish this semester. In only about four months, we have to get you to completely forget most of the useless and self-destructive information people have been telling you is true, factual, real, and 'good for you.' Then we have to teach you what's really important to know in order to have the life you want."

"Isn't that brainwashing?" one of the class shouted as a hush fell over the entire auditorium.

"Brainwashing. Well, yeah, I suppose it is," the professor answered laughing. "But not in the sense you would be thinking it to be. When you think of brainwashing, you are probably thinking of convincing someone of something against their will. It's a lot like some of these people who have showed up in recent years who are chasing some comet in order to be saved and led to 'the Promised Land.' Or entrenching themselves in some remote area of Texas or Arkansas, like on the beaches of Normandy, with more military power than Saddam Hussein. They claim to be 'messengers of God' or 'Messiahs' or some other euphemistic name for a self-serving individual who manipulates the hell out of people simply to serve his own ego. No, my friends, we shall not be brainwashing you like that. You've got to admit though, that most of your adolescent little brains could use a bit of a scrubbing!"

The class broke out in laughter. It was clear the students marveled not only in Professor McIntry's wit, but in his obvious passion as well. Each of the class, in their unique way, knew they were in for a semester unlike anything they had ever experienced.

"That question was important, and thank you to whomever asked it. It was important because it was probably a difficult question for that young man to ask. Why? Because it directly challenged what I was saying. I encourage you to challenge everything I will share with you, to explore it fully, without being so quick to accept it. I want you to hear me very clearly when I say this—" and he paused, then spoke louder, "always understand that you have the right to question anything you may be learning, especially when you are speaking about how to live your life. This is indeed your life, my friends. Be slow moving to accept anything—even the ideas that I will share with you—unless you can fully understand and accept them as your own."

"So you want us to question everything you say?" asked another student.

"I want you to question that which you do not understand. I want you to explore the answers to those questions that keep you up at night. I want you to question anything that, when you hear it, gives you that weird feeling in the pit of your stomach. That feeling that there is something more you need to discover. I want you to question *why* someone believes what he or she believes, including me. Most of the time we go through life just accepting the endless amount of information and data bombarding our senses. We accept all that information as true. Who says so? Who says you shouldn't go swimming right after you eat?"

While laughing with the class, the professor began again. "A simple and silly example, I agree, but that's just the beginning. Think of how many things, just like the swimming example, we have been taught or told over the years, by whomever may have been speaking, and now we live our lives by those ideas as if they were absolute truths.

"I would go as far as to say," the professor added, "that most of you have very few thoughts that are your own. You call yourselves original! What a joke! If it's not your parent's story you bought into, it's your teacher's. Or it's MTV's story or the newspaper's story or the government's story. More than likely, it is almost anyone's story but your own! Now, I am sure that some of you who consider yourselves to be 'rebels' or 'free thinkers' are starting to get pissed off and say, 'Not me. I think for myself.' Do you really? Do you really, now? So why are you a rebel and are those thoughts really of your own origination?

Or are they simply thoughts that conform to another group altogether, the 'rebel' group? Are you not much like your other friends who are 'rebels' too?"

"So how do we break free from that, professor?" Cole asked. "How do we get out from under the thoughts of these other sources when we are exposed to them all of the time?"

"It's a good question. And it's a question we will spend a lot of time talking about this semester," replied the professor. "Hold onto that for a minute; we will certainly come back to it.

"Okay, this reminds me. As a side note, since we are all on this journey together, I'd like to bring some form of togetherness and intimacy to this enormous group. What I would like is for you to take a moment or two before and after each class to introduce yourself to the other students in the class. Who knows, you might meet someone pretty cool. And please come up and introduce yourself to me as well, either here or in my office. I don't always remember names being shouted out, but I always remember them when I can attach them to a face. So make that a point, please. We might as well start now. What is your name?" the professor asked as he turned back to Cole.

"My name is Cole Anderson, sir."

"Very good, Mr. Anderson. And although I am still waiting for the queen to select me—and I, for one, believe I am long overdue—I haven't been knighted by Her Royal Highness just yet. And this isn't the military, so there is no need to address me as 'sir.' 'Professor,' 'Professor McIntry,' 'Elias,' or 'Eli' will all work just fine. 'Asshole,' 'bastard,' or 'unfair piece of crap' will likely be more appropriate at other times throughout the semester, but let's just stay with the suggested ones, shall we?" the professor added as a roar of laughter echoed through the lecture hall.

"Fellow journeyman, Cole Anderson has asked a very good question indeed. We will be exploring answers to it throughout the coming weeks. To start though, the fact that you have a desire to know the answer is the best place to begin. Accomplishment and achievement are born out of desire. Desire is fuel for the engines of our minds and souls. Without it, we fall into apathy and are plagued by indecision. And worst of all, we suffer a slow and painful living death, as if being buried alive with a small window we can see out of. We become victims to one of the most prevalent thieves of personal self-worth and confidence known to man: procrastination. So keep rich your desire to find the truth in everything, to explore the make-up of your own soul and the jigsaw puzzle of belief systems that make you who you are.

"So, why don't we have a textbook for this class?" he asked and then paused. "Because I didn't feel like writing one. That's why!" the professor added, chuckling. "While part of that may be true, the more valid reason is just as simple. This class, as is your life, is about you. It's about you starting to discover who you really are and what the hell you are doing in this marvelous playground we have to enjoy called Earth. As we all walk together in this world, each of us walks separately, each forming our own opinions and beliefs and thoughts that make up our own reality. Some of our opinions may be shared by others and some may be all our own. Nevertheless, they are only ever just our opinions. So how do we write a textbook that can change and adapt for each and every fellow journeyman who decides to take this class? It's very simple. Just like life, we make it up as we go along. Moment by moment, day by day, week by week…we will create the textbook for this class, and thus for your life.

"As far as grades, you all get an A." The professor was interrupted by a wave of applause and shouting from the class. Continuing, he said, "Although if you want to keep that A, it is up to you. Just like in your life, my friends, you will be graded on your participation and your results. As always, how well you do is entirely your choice. If you participate, if you are prepared to learn, grow, and challenge yourself, then at the end of the semester, that A will still be yours. Skip class, fall asleep, keep silent, don't do your assignments, or do anything else you usually do to try to slide your way right through a class, and I will gladly slide you right past those good grades.

"All right, this seems like a good enough place as any to call it a day. Before you go, please jot down this assignment to complete for next week. In one hundred words or less, answer the question, 'Who am I?'—the question that man has been asking for thousands of years. The question that, when combined with its counterpart 'Why am I here?,' has formed the basis for most of our modern-day religions, as well as ancient philosophy and wisdom. For the time being, we'll focus on you. Let's see if together we can discover who you really are.

"I understand this one-hundred-word limit will likely be a challenge for some of your ever so overinflated egos. After all, the subject matter is your ego's favorite thing to discuss: yourselves. Please be careful. As you begin this assignment, be aware that your ego is a powerful foe, my friends, and it seeks to take control and serve itself whenever you'll let it. You will have a tendency to discuss who you think you ought to be, or who others see you as, or who you portray yourself to be. Hell, some of the guys in here might even buy into one of the stories they used last week at the pub on some unexpecting, well-intentioned young lady," the professor continued over the laughter of the class.

"Needless to say, none of that will serve you or the assignment. You must dig deep, young warriors. We are here together, seeking the truth. And I will be so bold as to say that the truth of who you really are is deep within the confines of your soul. It's more than likely hidden away so deep no one else can see it, guarded from the outside world by your well-maintained shield of security. This self-constructed shield of yours helps to protect your ego by maintaining its status, its power, and its perception of self. It's very possible you may come face to face with the person whom you haven't known for years, perhaps since you had the innocence of a young child. It's also possible this is the person who only comes out when it's safe, when he or she knows they aren't susceptible to the infections that so commonly plague our world. So yes indeed, my little journeymen, dig deep. The success of your semester, as well as the inner harmony you wish to create in your life, lay on the shoulders of this assignment.

"I want to encourage you not to share your answers or to discuss the question at all with anyone else. If you choose not to adhere to my suggestion and you don't do this assignment by yourself, you will end up getting more of what we have already discussed—a life led by thoughts that are not your own. So please put your own thought into it because it is in that way, and only in that way, your answer will serve to be of any benefit at all.

"Until next week, my fellow journeymen. It's been wonderful to meet you. My office hours and phone number are on the board behind me. Come to class next week prepared to play the game. And remember, in the game of life anything can happen, and usually does," Professor McIntry said as he walked out the side door of the lecture hall, leaving the class in a daze, half of them not knowing what just happened and the other half stunned by his brilliance.

Cole, Hope, and Jake looked at each other, finished taking down the notes from the board, got up, and silently made their way out to the courtyard. They lay down on the grass, taking in the warmth of the midday sun and feeling alive like never before.

CHAPTER SEVEN

Crack. The sound echoed through the stadium like a gunshot. As the ball caromed off the wall in left center, Pete rounded first and slid into second base beating the throw in from left field. It was perfect weather for the SCSU Titan's first home game of the season. The wind blew ever so gently and made for a mild Southern California winter day of about sixty-eight degrees.

Baseball wasn't SCSU's sport of top priority, which was reflected by the second-class stadium. Although the field could have used a complete overhaul, they managed to keep it in the best condition they could. Nevertheless, there was a festive atmosphere of cheers and high-fives in the stands. Even the wave found its way into the stadium that afternoon. None of the gang would have missed this game for the world. Pete's first college game. They were probably all as excited to watch him, as he was to play. Hope and Cole cheered for their friend as Pete asked the second base umpire for timeout to dust himself off. Jake had asked Susan to join them, thinking he wouldn't be nearly as nervous on a date with his friends there.

Susan had a very natural, beautiful look about her. She was one of those people who looked very comfortable in her own skin. She didn't need the assistance of a lot of makeup and rarely wore any. Cole and Hope instantly liked her. Although all three of them were just getting to know her, it was obvious Susan had a huge heart and still believed people were, in essence, good. In many ways, she was like a more grown-up version of Hope.

Jake hadn't stopped thinking about her since the previous weekend. He tried to stay in control of his emotions and was doing the best he could, but he had never met anyone like Susan before. Although Pete would have advised him to hold back his feelings and stay in control, he just didn't care. He didn't understand why she had such an impact on him. They had only been together for about an hour in the bar and had spoken on the phone twice, but she always made Jake feel so wonderful. She was indeed special. Something inside of Jake told him they were supposed to meet. As Susan glanced back from the field, she caught Jake staring at her.

Startled, and not knowing if she would be flattered or think he was a psycho, he quickly asked, "Do you remember Pete from th-th-the other night? You didn't really get to meet him, but he was the g-g-guy who came up to me and told me he was leaving."

"Yeah, I remember. So that's him, number twenty-four?" Susan inquired.

"Yeah, that's him. He's the only freshman st-sta-starting for varsity this year," Jake added.

"You've got to give him credit. He worked his ass off to make varsity," said Cole as he watched Pete play in front of a healthy crowd of about six hundred.

"Yeah, he told enough women he had the starting job long before it was actually his," said Jake. "I guess it was inevitable it would come true. You're right, though. He has worked hard. God knows he would rather have been down in Cabo with us, or even just relaxing at home."

"I'm proud of him," Hope started in. "He really focused this time. You know we couldn't have always said that about Pete. Who would have thought our Pete would be the starting shortstop for varsity baseball at State? I think it's pretty cool. I really am proud of him."

"When did you go to Cabo?" Susan jumped in and asked. "Did all of you go?"

"We went down when Christmas break let out. It was just the three of us 'cause Pete had practice. We only stayed a couple days, but it was an incredible trip," Hope replied.

For a moment, Hope, Cole, and Jake were silent, back on the beach, dreaming under the stars. The feeling was so strong it was like they had been there just a few hours ago. Perhaps it was because it had been the first time they had talked together about important life issues. Generally Cole and Jake talked about sports, or partying, or music, or women. The conversation rarely got philosophical and they hardly ever talked about the future, unless they were referring to the upcoming weekend. Or maybe it was because of Professor McIntry's class and the things he had said. Maybe they felt strange because the class seemed to be answering some of the questions Cole had voiced on the beach that night.

"Hey, Pete just scored!" Susan shouted, jumping up to cheer for the Titans and snapping the three of them out of the nostalgic daze they had fallen into.

"Whoooooooooaaaaaaaaaaa!" they chanted simultaneously.

"Go Pete! Go Titans!" screamed Hope at the top of her lungs.

"What did you think about the class today, guys? He seems like an incredible teacher, doesn't he?" asked Hope, as she shifted her thoughts back to where they had been before the excitement of Pete's scoring.

"'Incredible' isn't even the right word. I've never had a teacher like that before," Cole stated. "In fact, I don't think I've ever met anyone like that before. He's got so much life and knowledge, and he's hilarious."

"Yeah, you've got that right. I'm so glad I got in, Jake added.

"You ended up taking the class?" asked Susan enthusiastically. "That's fantastic. I knew there was something I liked about you," and she gave him a big hug.

Smiling, Jake looked back at Hope and Cole and said in a coy voice, "Well, uh, are there any other classes you'd like me t-t-to take?" and they all had a big laugh.

"Jake, you know, I noticed something. Did you realize you only stutter when you are speaking directly to me? You haven't been stuttering when you talk to Cole or Hope," Susan pointed out.

"When you first met me, Jake, I think I remember you used to stutter when you talked to me, didn't you?" Hope said.

"That's 'cause he had a secret crush on you," Cole jumped in. "You used to make him so nervous he couldn't even say your name. It was hysterical."

"Yeah, real fucking funny," Jake said, not finding the humor in it.

"Oh, come on, Jake," Cole continued. "You remember when I first introduced you to Hope. We were…what? Freshmen in high school, right? Anyway, when I introduced you, you were stuttering so bad you just ran out of the school. Susan, you should have seen him. It was like the place was on fire."

Jake looked at Cole and cracked a bit of a grin. Then Cole said, "I mean, if we didn't end up staying friends, or you weren't this cool man we see here today who I love like a brother, it might have been kinda sad. But you've got to admit it, Jake. Looking back at it now, its all pretty damn funny."

"I think it's really interesting," Susan said. "So you only stutter around women you aren't comfortable with, or who you have feelings for, or who make you nervous? I guess it will be fun getting to know you well enough so that I don't make you nervous anymore. Jake, remember in the bar last week? Did you ever wonder why I asked you how long you've had your stutter?"

"I guess I ne-ne-never really thought about it," Jake replied.

"It's because until I was seventeen, Jake, I stuttered too," admitted Susan.

"G-g-get out of here!" Jake stammered.

"Really, you had a stutter, Susan?" Hope asked.

"Yeah, it was about like Jake's. I only really stuttered when I got nervous. When I was young, though, I was a pretty shy kid, so I got nervous a lot. It was awful. Jake, you know how it is when you're young. Kids can be so cruel. They think your stutter is the funniest thing going, and they never miss an opportunity to make fun of you," Susan replied. Jake nodded his head obviously remembering some of those days from his youth he would rather just forget. She continued. "I worked with a speech coach and a psychotherapist. I found out my stuttering was really nothing more than a mental block. I had some repressed emotions and feelings from when I was growing up. Once I resolved those issues within myself, the stuttering was gone."

"That's great, Jake, isn't it? I mean, there's a possibility you could rid yourself of your stutter. That's fantastic," Hope said, happy for her friend.

"Yeah, I guess. I don't exactly see what's so great about it, though. Hell, if there are repressed emotions, they are probably repressed for a pretty good reason. I don't think it sounds too fantastic to go back and relive whatever crap caused my stuttering in the first place. I can think of better ways to spend an afternoon," Jake said sarcastically.

"I'll help you if you want, Jake. It's up to you. You will learn a lot of things about yourself in Professor McIntry's class this semester, and you may discover what it is that's causing it, all on your own. All I know is, if you don't deal with your past and work through it to where you make peace with whatever caused you pain, it's going to resurface time and time again," said Susan, understanding what Jake was feeling. "Like I said, it's up to you. I want you to know though, that I will be here for you if you decide to work on it."

"I'll think about it, Susan," Jake said. "Thanks. Really, I mean it, thanks a lot. First the beer, then this," he added as he leaned over and pinched her in the arm.

"Ouch, what was that for?"

"I was just making sure you were real," Jake said, transforming Susan's puzzled look into a huge smile.

Susan had a smile that instantly brought warmth to a cold day. It reflected the tenderness of her heart and the gentleness of her soul. It was comforting and safe, and made everything seem like it was going to be okay even though the world around you seemed chaotic.

Cole and Hope smiled at each other. They were impressed with Susan and the obvious connection she felt with Jake. Cole knew Jake was excited about Susan as well—he could always tell when Jake liked a girl. Jake rarely got emotional about women, mainly because he didn't meet a whole lot of them. But when he liked someone, his eyes glazed over as though he was in another world altogether, whenever they were together. And right now Jake's eyes were in full-glaze mode.

Pete was up one more time in the bottom of the eighth inning. He swung at the first pitch and hit a screaming line drive that took one hop before bouncing off the right center field fence. Pete hustled into second with a stand-up double and went on to score later in the inning. The Titans finished with a commanding victory, by a spread of six to one. Pete proved to be one of the stars in his first game ever as a Titan, going three for four and making a fantastic diving grab that saved a run in the fifth inning.

"Oh, he's gonna be celebrating for all it's worth tonight, no doubt," said Cole admiring his friend's performance in the game. "My friends, I am in the mood for a good *fiesta*. Would you like to join us, Susan?"

"Thanks, Cole, but I think I can ask her myself," Jake barked. "Would you like to join us?" he asked laughing.

"I'd really like that. Thanks," she replied.

It was about half past twelve and the Titans' victory celebration was in full swing. The party was at one of the senior players' houses and it was packed as full as you could get it. The crowd overflowed into the backyard, with people wandering aimlessly. It was a typical college male's home: a rented three-bedroom occupied by five guys and decorated with a distasteful array of mix-and-match furniture, most of which had been inherited from graduating friends. The music thumped at deafening levels, interrupted only by the occasional and completely unnecessary display of displaced testosterone.

Pete sat on a plaid tweed couch in the corner with a cute little redhead under one arm, a sexy blond under the other, a beer between his legs and a toothy smile to make any self-respecting dentist proud. "Gotta love it. Hitting seven-fifty right out of the box. Whoooaaaaaa!" Pete exclaimed, reliving the day's all-star–like moments.

"He likes to talk about himself a lot, huh?" Susan commented half jokingly.

"The way I see it, we'll take it easy on him tonight and let him do whatever the hell he wants. I mean, look at him. He's in his own little heaven. He's shit-faced, and he's got not one but two beautiful women draped all over him and thinking he's none other than God Himself," said Cole. "Hell, he deserves it, he had a frickin' awesome game today. Besides, if he gets drunk enough, he's bound to do something extremely stupid we'll be able to use against him later."

"As he usually does. Hey, anyone want a beer?" asked Jake, making his way to the kitchen. The three of them nodded "yes."

"So Jake tells me all of you have been friends for a pretty long time. I think it's great. It's rare to stick together so long," Susan said.

"The three *amigos* here have been causing trouble together since they were little tykes," Hope responded. "They've been inseparable for as long as anyone can remember. They grew up in the same neighborhood and have always gone to school together, as far as I know. I met Cole and then Pete and Jake when we were fourteen."

"Yeah, Pete and I went to preschool together, if you can believe that," said Cole. "We met Jake a couple years later in second grade, which is really when all hell broke loose. Jake has always been the perfect balance for us. If you haven't noticed, Pete and I are kinda crazy. Well, I've settled down a bit since Hopes and I have been together, more so in the last year. But man, we were always causing some sort of trouble. Hell, Pete and I probably would be dead by now if it weren't for Jake. He's always been that anchor we needed," Cole added. "Jake is the reason all of us have stayed together so long. So treat him right, Susan. Jake's as good as they come. He's all heart."

"Yeah, Jake's the best," Hope chimed in. "He really is."

"I am beginning to see that," Susan replied.

"To the Titans!" shouted Pete, standing and raising his beer high in the air.

Jake made it back from the beer run just in time to join the entire party toast: "To the Titans!"

As night turned into dawn, people were either crashed on the sofa or in a back bedroom, stumbling their way across campus to their own homes, or still partying with no conception of the time. The motley crew of guests had consumed enough alcohol to float a battleship. Pete had been busy flirting with both of his newfound friends. The best part for Pete was neither one of them seemed to mind the other. Hope, Jake, and Susan were sitting in the backyard telling stories about growing up—the good ones, the bad ones, and the ones they would just as soon forget. The truth serum called Miller Lite had dissolved their inhibitions and helped them open up to each other.

Hope spoke of growing up with just one parent after her mother had died, which they came to find out was similar to Susan's situation. Although Susan's mother hadn't passed away, she too had been raised by her father. Her mother had left her father for another man when Susan was ten. Susan tracked her down when she was seventeen. After some good old-fashioned yelling and screaming, they had worked through their difficulties and now had a wonderful relationship. Jake got bold enough to tell Susan about his parents' recent decision to get a divorce, although he didn't go into any details on the horrors of growing up in the war zone they called a family.

"Hey, where's Cole?" Hope asked.

"I haven't seen him in a while," Jake replied.

"Neither have I," added Susan.

Meanwhile, in the front yard Cole sat leaning against the trunk of a tree. The ground glistened with moisture in anticipation of a new day's arrival. He was hammered from the many rounds of toasting "the Titans," "old friends," "new friends," "friends they haven't met yet," "going three-for-four," "diving catches," "stuttering," "not stuttering," and any other excuse to drink up.

"Who am I?" he said aloud, but to himself, remembering the assignment from Professor McIntry. "Who is Cole Anderson? I am...I am...I am da man! Yeah, that's right...I am da man! Cole is da man," he said laughing out loud as if he were alone on a deserted island. "No, okay, get serious. Who am I? Who am I? I am one drunk son of a bitch, that's who I am! Drunk as a skunk I am! Okay...serious now," he said, but he couldn't stop laughing. "Who am I? Cole Anderson is like that distant star up in the sky..." He pointed his finger aimlessly into the air. "...shining bright, but no one knows what he's really about."

When he was under the influence, Cole's mood swung predictably from laughter to one of complete seriousness. "A shining example for others to follow, yet not knowing where the hell he's going or how to get there.... All I know is I don't have a fucking clue who I am! What the hell kind of question is that anyway? Who am I? Who the hell are you, Professor McIntry? Who are you to ask a question like that? What have *you* done to give you the right to ask such a question? Yeah, who the hell are you, Professor Elias McIntry?"

Cole was getting louder now. "A pretty frickin' funny dude, Eli. That's who you are," he said as his emotions swung back to the lighter side. "A funny dude who dresses funny and doesn't brush his hair and probably smells of BO.... But as funny as you may be, oh, fellow journeyman McIntry, I still don't know how to answer your damn question. Help me out, stars," Cole requested looking up into the sky. "Who is Cole Anderson? Who am I other than a crazy bastard who likes to talk to the stars?" he said not realizing that he had hit full volume.

Flanked by Susan and Hope, Jake approached his friend. "Where's that magic hammock when you need it? Huh, Cole?" he said.

Startled, Cole struggled to compose himself. "You said it, bruddha! The magic hammock. Where's that magic hammock when you need it?" he said. "But-ah-um-ah, how long have you guys been standing there?"

"Since about 'Who the hell are you, professor?'," said Jake.

"Great. That's just wonderful. So now you've all had your suspicions confirmed. I'm completely frickin' nuts," Cole said, feeling self-conscious.

"Hey, it's not like we don't all understand exactly where you're coming from," said Hope. "How well do any of us know ourselves, whether we want to admit it or not? I'd like to think I do, but then why do I still get upset too easily, or worry, or don't stand up for myself sometimes? I think we all have questions about who we are."

"I've got to admit though, you looked pretty funny shouting to the sky. You would have thought you were trying to make it rain or something," Jake said, laughing. "You'll figure it out, buddy. We'll all figure it out. Maybe not today, or tomorrow, but we will. What do you say we call it a night? Who's ready for dreamtime?"

"Do you want to get Pete before we go?" Hope asked.

"Something tells me Pete's already living his dream. He's got two women—I think he'll be fine. We'll catch up to him tomorrow," Cole said, getting up. "Okay, let's get outta here." And the four of them went off down the street, heading back home.

As they walked along with their arms around each other, they thought about their lives, the direction they were taking, and how it all fit together. The sun came up behind them as if signifying the dawning of not just a new day, but of a new time. A time when it seemed like the days stretched on for weeks, and everything that happened had a huge significance that would impact their destinies. It was a time to rejoice in old friends and welcome new ones. It was a time for Jake to break free from feelings of inadequacy and Cole to leave an internal life filled with self-condemnation and sabotaging behavior. It was a time when they all understood the value of having true friends. And as they walked down the street together, they stepped into the dawning of a world between the worlds. They all felt it. They all knew it.

CHAPTER EIGHT

"Our deepest fear is not that we are inadequate. Our deepest fear is that we are powerful beyond measure," Professor McIntry bellowed as the students took their seats and became silent to begin class. "It is our light, not our darkness, that most frightens us. We ask ourselves, 'Who am I to be brilliant, gorgeous, talented, fabulous?' Actually, who are you not to be? You are a child of God. Your playing small doesn't serve the world. There's nothing enlightened about shrinking so other people won't feel insecure around you. We are all meant to shine as children do. We are born to manifest the glory of God that is within us. It is not just in some of us. It's in everyone. And as we let our light shine, we unconsciously give other people permission to do the same."

He paused, collected the energy that was building in the silence of the lecture hall, and continued speaking, even louder and more forceful than before. As his voice became more commanding, he spoke the words of Marianne Williamson, which were later made more famous by Nelson Mandela. The professor seemed almost luminescent as he said, "As we're liberated from our own fears, our presence automatically liberates others."

Professor McIntry stood in front of the class looking down at the paper in front of him. Two hundred and fifteen college students focused one hundred percent of their energy toward the professor. The speech had gotten them. They hadn't simply listened to the words as he spoke; they had really felt the message. The meaning penetrated right through to their souls.

"So how is your spirit, class?" he asked.

"Inspired!" someone shouted.

"Wonderful. Now, what kind of emotions does that short yet powerful speech bring up in you?" asked the professor.

There was dead silence in the room. The students sat there dazed or too nervous to speak out or thinking of clever ways to answer. Still others were lost.

"Come on! How did that make you feel?" the professor asked again.

"My name is Laurie Kaufman, professor. It made me feel excited and enthused. I could picture that speech being given in front of a huge crowd. It was inspiring."

"Thank you, Laurie. Who else?"

"Jake Nelson, Professor McIntry."

"Go ahead, Jake. What did you take from that speech?"

"I didn't get the sense of a big crowd at all. I felt like you were talking directly to me. I felt like you were saying 'Hey, Jake, get over your fears and start living.' I agree that it was inspiring, but it was also kind of depressing, knowing that you could be or should be more than you are," Jake said.

"Fantastic, both of you," commented the professor enthusiastically. "This exercise, or anything else we'll do here, is not meant to depress you. Although it is certainly meant to get you to think. Perhaps thinking is something many of you choose not to do a lot of. Of course, you have every right to make that choice. But I assure you that forward thinking is crucial for you, not only to receive a successful grade in this class, but also for you to have the reward of a fulfilling and satisfying existence on this planet.

"Mr. Nelson, would you agree it is only depressing if you feel you actually can't do anything about it? So often when we take a close look at ourselves and how our life is going, it's necessary to experience a moment of dissatisfaction in order for us to get off our proverbial asses and get to the point where we can make the decision to change. So, it can only be a lasting depression if you either don't know how to change or feel powerless to change, agreed?"

Jake nodded in agreement. Then Cole spoke up.

"But what can we do about it, sir? Ah, I mean, professor. What can we really do about it? I am nineteen years old. What power do I have to do much of anything? To me, that speech talked about greatness...what could I possibly do right now to be great? It just seems so far removed from where life is. I mean, I go to school, hang out with friends, and party. And at the same time, I try not to get too caught up in all the pressures that go along with it all."

"Ah, but, Cole, do you not feel there is something else beyond the day-to-day activities that make up your life?" the professor asked.

Somehow he knew. Somehow the professor knew Cole had been questioning everything and everyone as to their realness. And more than anything else, he knew he had been questioning himself, his own existence, and this whole damn seeming merry-go-round of emotions that made up his life.

"I sure as hell hope so!" Cole exclaimed.

"My fellow journeymen, I want to tell you something that may seem discouraging to some of you; and to others it may even seem a bit cruel. You see, unfortunately, most of you won't understand many of the messages this class is working to teach. Sure, you may finish up with good enough grades, but you won't have taken with you the real lessons behind our work here. 'Why is that?' you may ask," the professor continued. "Because you don't want to. That's the real truth of it. This class is going to show you how to deal with a world most people don't talk about. It's a world most people are afraid of. It's a world many people refuse to admit has any real significance. My friends, we are talking about your internal world. We are talking about the state of affairs that makes up the workings of your mind: all the feelings that twist and turn inside you, all the inner dialogue you have with yourself constantly, and with all the years of past programming you have to sift through when trying to tackle a new experience. It's the place where we define our self-image, from where we draw our confidence, and where we can overcome our feelings of self-doubt, unworthiness, insecurity, and fear.

"Most of you won't get it because you are too fixated on the world around you, as opposed to the world within you. Most of you are too caught up in thinking about how much money you will make, or what kind of neat stuff you will own, or the kind of car you will drive, or the important job title you will have. Yes…most of you are so caught up in all of that bullshit, that it's almost impossible for you to be concerned with the type of person you can become. How do I know? It's because the odds are against you. Nearly every piece of information you receive out in the world tells you the key to life is having more stuff than everyone else. They say that money and money alone will bring you happiness, that fame and fortune are more important than integrity and peace of mind, and that external beauty means internal happiness. What a crock!

"My friends, we live in a world that is addicted to the accomplishments of the ego. The lives of people who are considered icons in the public's view are made out to be all glitz and glamour. The real prizes and valuable lessons are the stories of what those same icons had to work through in order to get to where they are now. The pains they had to deal with, the obstacles they had to overcome, the sacrifices they had to make, the countless nights it took every last ounce of their courage not to simply throw in the towel and say 'to hell with it all.' Those are the stories we can learn from.

"Some of you may think what I've just shared with you is a pessimistic view. You may ask why I teach this class if I believe only so few of those I teach will even get the message. To that question I would say it is for those special few who *are* willing to learn that I stand here before you today. You see, my friends, it is the few who step beyond the rest, the few who call on reserves of power they did not know they had, who will undoubtedly change the world. It only takes one person talking loudly enough and long enough to influence the lives of millions. It has always been the case—from Nelson Mandela, to Mahatma Gandhi, to Dr. King, to Jesus Himself, and it will always be that way. I have already made the choice as to what my life's purpose is, my role in the evolution of this great planet. The choice you have to make for yourself is what side of the fence you wish to be on."

Pausing a moment to let his message sink in, the professor added, "To get back to your question, Mr. Anderson, greatness is not an external quality, it is an internal discipline. We must first become great human beings before we can accomplish great feats and indeed, no age is too early to become a great human being. Something tells me you are already on your way."

"Well now that we have your juices flowing this morning, let's get back to the question I asked you last week, shall we?" the professor continued. "The long sought-after yet rarely found answer to the question that burns deep inside us all, 'Who am I?' How many people had difficulty answering this question?" he asked and nearly every hand in the room went up. "Who wants to share some of their experiences?"

"My name is Angel Graham, Professor McIntry."

"Go ahead, Angel."

"Who am I? I am a strong, powerful, compassionate, loving, independent, friendly, outgoing, funny, intelligent, and secure black woman."

"Thank you, Angel. Indeed, you are. Anyone else?"

"My name is Colin Whitsfield. I am the pissed-off son of a wealthy father who has run my entire life since the day I was born."

"Ah…that's good, Colin. Thanks. And I promise I won't tell your father. You'll get more out of this class than you think, if you pay attention. Thanks for sharing that," the professor said. "Fantastic. Okay, everyone. Who or what has been the major influences that have helped shape your personality? Who or what has been the biggest factors that have caused you to become the person who you are?"

"Parents," someone said.

"Teachers," shouted another.

"Good, great." The professor said enthusiastically as he wrote down their responses on the overhead projector and flashed it up on the big screen behind him. "What else?"

"Our friends," added Jake.

"Churches and religions," someone else commented.

"How about the media!" another student tossed in.

"Now we're getting somewhere!" exclaimed Professor McIntry. "What else? Dig deep."

"Ourselves!" was shouted from the back of the class.

"Society," someone else said.

"The government," said a girl from the front row.

"The past," someone else shouted.

"Wonderful. Anything else?" the professor asked and the class was silent. "Good. This is a great start. Let's just say for the sake of example that these people and these groups were the only ones that influenced you. I am sure, given some more time, you could think of even more. But let's just use these. Are you beginning to see how much information is coming at you every day? Do you realize how much junk you have to sift through just to figure out what it is you really believe?

"Now, do you really think that each and every one of those people and organizations has had your best interest at heart?" the professor asked. "Or could they possibly have their own best interest at heart? The real trick, the real secret to this whole deal, is to be able to remove yourself from external influences and, at the same time, exist within them."

"Huh?" was shouted from the back of the room, followed by a burst of laughter.

"All right, let me explain what I mean. Let's say you decide the government, the media, and the religious entities of the world are really manipulating the hell out of most of the people in the world simply to heighten their own power. And so, you develop your own set of internal beliefs, very likely different from theirs, and you live your life by your beliefs. Unless you decide to go live in a cave on a remote island somewhere, you must figure out a way to live within the system, until the system changes to support your inner beliefs and ideals."

"Isn't that selling out?" asked a young black student from the front.

"No. I don't think so. In my opinion, selling out would be giving up what you believe to fit into the system. There's a big difference between that and figuring out how to live with your own beliefs within the system. Wouldn't you agree?" the professor asked and the student nodded.

"Half the reason the world is in the state it is in is because hardly anyone knows what they truly believe in anymore. And for the ones who do know what they believe in," the professor continued, "most of them don't have a clue as to why the hell they believe it. Most people bought into a story when they were growing up. Then that story was reconfirmed as they got older by nearly all the organizations and institutions they were associated with. Before they knew it, they were stuck so deep in the quicksand of 'system thinking' they didn't know how to get out.

"I don't have any concern for what someone believes. It doesn't matter to me if you are a Catholic or a Buddhist, an atheist or a metaphysical healer. I don't care whether you believe small green men come to visit you in the middle of the night or whether you like to cross-dress."

The class was amused by the professor's examples.

He continued. "It's amazing to me how people get so mad and frustrated when others have different beliefs. Look at all the wars fought over religious differences. People have been killing each other for years because they have different interpretations of God. It's all so damned silly, if you ask me. Their beliefs are just their opinions anyway, especially about God. Just think about it…arguing about what God means, when God just is. Well, we'll save that for later in the semester.

"But please, whatever you believe in, believe in something! Do yourself a favor, though—understand why you believe what you believe and make damn sure it supports you in your journey. There are far too many people who simply drift through life not caring about anything or anyone. Stand up, everyone. No, I mean literally, go ahead and stand up right now!" he shouted to the class and everyone stood up. "Wonderful, now you can all at least say you stand for something."

He laughed at his own pathetically comic example as the class sat back down. "Seriously though, when everything seems distant, out of focus or incomprehensible—or just when you think you have hit your boiling point and you just can't take any more—if you believe in nothing else, believe in yourself. Believe in your own infinite power to accomplish all you desire, do whatever you wish to do, and become whomever you wish to be. Because the truth, my fellow journeymen, is our life is but an unfolding story that we create in the depths of our own souls and in the recesses of our own minds. Indeed, we make it up as we go. Whether your story is joyous, fun, exciting, and rewarding or filled with misery, loneliness, and discord…it is all up to you. Because you, my friends, are the authors of your own book of life. So sharpen those pencils that are you minds and prepare yourself to write a masterpiece. Be elegant like Hemingway or Shakespeare, or be provoking like Thoureau or Emerson, or be a maverick like J. D. Salinger or one of my favorites, Stuart Wilde. But most of all, be that magnificent, creative, and inspired creature that is you!

"Okay, we have an assignment for next week. I want you to finish the sentence 'Happiness is…' Take as few words as you want. Please don't make it too long. In your own opinion, just finish that phrase. What is happiness to you?

"Please hand in your 'Who am I?' papers before you leave. See you next week."

CHAPTER NINE

"It's really great to get away for lunch like this, just the two of us, with no guys," Hope said to Susan as they sat at a rare outdoor table at The Tavern. "Don't get me wrong—I love the guys. But it's nice to have some time with just another woman."

"I know exactly what you mean. I had a boyfriend before Jake and when we started seeing each other, we were together all of the time. I don't have a lot of girlfriends, so it wasn't as though it took time away from that, but I missed time by myself. You know, 'me time,'" Susan commented.

"Yeah, I don't think most guys understand 'me time' too well. I don't think it makes sense to them," Hope laughed. "They always have to be doing something. It's so funny. Cole's that way, except for recently. He's been spending a lot of time by himself lately, but he's going through intense self-observation right now, which I think is good. So you and Jake have been spending a lot of time together recently, haven't you?"

"A pretty good amount. I think he's fantastic. He's so genuine and innocent, yet at the same time he has a subtle wisdom to him. It's so rare to find a guy who has strength of character, yet isn't afraid to show you his heart. I really enjoy spending time with him," Susan added.

"I just love Jake. He really is a great guy. All three of them are so special to me. We've been through so much together. Back when we were in high school, we used to skip classes sometimes and go out to the lake all day and get a baked-on tan while we just talked and talked. Pete and Jake have always talked to me about all their dates and girl problems," Hope reminisced. "I remember the weekend Jake lost his virginity!"

They both laughed as the waiter came over to take their lunch order. It was another picture-perfect day in San Diego County. There was a slight breeze and the sun had warmed the air to seventy degrees. Hope continued to share stories with Susan about high school experiences and her father. Hope's father played a very special role in her life. After her mother died, Hope became close to her father, and she cherished their relationship. In a lot of ways, she took on her mother's role. Even the relationship she had with the boys was very maternal, and she recognized that.

"And what about yourself, Hope? How is everything going for you? It seemed you had something specific you wanted to talk to me about when you asked me to lunch. What was it?" Susan asked.

"Gosh, I know Jake said you were pretty perceptive," Hope replied. "I guess-um-ah, not really anything specific. I don't know."

As Hope groped for her thoughts, the waiter brought their food. Hope looked up and smiled, they ate and she gently switched the subject. Susan realized there was something Hope had to get out, but she decided to give her the space she needed. So, over lunch they talked about Susan's background and her plans for after college.

As they were finishing up, Hope said, "I guess there are some things that have been bothering me," then paused to collect her thoughts. Hope was so used to helping other people and being there for them when they needed it, that she didn't often talk about how she felt, or what was going on inside of her. Although she was uncomfortable, she wanted to talk. She needed to talk. And finally, she had another girl to talk with. She was glad it was Susan there with her. Although they had only met a few weeks before, they had begun to develop a good friendship. Susan was true, not just to others, but most importantly to herself. Hope respected the fact that Susan wouldn't tell you what you wanted to hear; she'd tell you the truth. She could ask difficult questions and be okay about it, and you wouldn't feel she was being rude. Susan had said many times that Professor McIntry's class had changed her life. Whatever it had done for her, it had done it well.

"I guess I have just been having these feelings about myself lately," Hope started in. "A lot of it has to do with Cole and me. I mean, I love Cole—I really do—and things have gotten so much better. But—" and she paused. It was obvious she was holding back her emotions and that this was tough for her.

"But what, Hope? It's okay, really," Susan prompted.

"I know he's cheated on me a couple times. I guess I just convinced myself he'd grow out of it and that it wasn't important. But I'm having a harder time dealing with it than I thought. It's like I have always been there for these guys for everything, and I know I've helped them a lot—especially Cole, to help him discover who he really is and what he's all about. I've always been able to see through that big ego of his."

Susan chuckled in understanding.

"It's like I've spent so much time concerned with them, that I've forgotten to take care of me" Hope continued. " I mean, what kind of woman lets her boyfriend sleep with other women without getting thoroughly pissed off? I must be absolutely crazy."

"You are definitely not crazy, Hope, well, not any more than the rest of us," Susan responded. "Is it so bad that you're such a good friend to these guys, helping them, being there for them, and giving them a shoulder to cry on?"

"No, of course not. I guess it's just that, well, I guess I feel I've hurt myself in the process. You know, giving out great advice but not doing it myself," Hope said.

"Sounds like you are tired of filling your mom's shoes. I mean, that's what all this is really about, isn't it?" Susan said boldly. "Look, you've surrounded yourself with men who need you, and need you a lot. Don't get me wrong, that's not really a bad thing. We could both think of a lot of things that would be worse than being surrounded by three attractive men. But sometimes it's easy to care so much about helping people who are important to you that you forget to take care of yourself. My mother was the same way; it was part of the reason she left us. It took her over thirty-five years to figure that out. But it looks like you're doing it in half the time."

That brought a smile to Hope's face; on the inside, her mind was racing. Was it too late to change things? Was Cole going to continue to cheat on her? How would he like it if she stood up for herself more? So many thoughts and questions bounced back and forth in her mind, and she felt a bit overwhelmed.

"It's okay, Hope," consoled Susan, sensing that Hope was getting upset. "It will all work out; it always does. I know it probably seems like you're running on overload right now, huh?"

Hope nodded as she held back her tears.

"Hey, remember when you were in high school," Susan asked, "how everything was such a major deal? If you heard one of the girls say something bad about you or you didn't get invited to a party, it was like the world was going to end. Well, emotions run just as strong now, just about different things. But you made it through all those things in high school, and you'll make it through this."

"Yeah, I know. I'm upset because it's a lot to deal with and mad at myself for letting it get to this point," Hope said. "I guess I've known for a while that things weren't exactly right inside me, but I guess I just couldn't figure it out."

"Hey, remember how I described Jake?" asked Susan. "'He has strength of character but is also willing to show his heart.'"

"Yeah."

"Well, it's a pretty attractive combination in anyone. You have it, Hope, and now you know it. I'm excited for you. This is a big breakthrough," Susan remarked.

"You know, you're right! You are absolutely right! Susan, thank you so much. I can't tell you how much talking to you has helped me. You can't have learned all this from Professor McIntry's class," Hope said and a big, bright smile turned up the corners of her mouth.

"Well, like I told you guys at the game, when I overcame my stuttering, I went through some major things from my past and learned how to deal with them. But the professor's class gave me a completely different outlook on the world." Susan paused. "It gave me the confidence to be myself."

They paid the bill, got up to leave and hugged each other like old friends who hadn't seen each other in years. They had created a bond that would prove to be a special relationship for both of them. Although they hugged only for a moment, it seemed to take away all the uneasiness Hope had been feeling and a beautiful sense of peace came over her. She had indeed made a breakthrough, and she had Susan to thank for it.

"You two aren't leaving, are you?" said Cole as he approached with Pete and Jake.

Wiping her face to make sure the tears were gone Hope said, "Well, we were about to, but—"

"Stay with us. We're going to have a beer," Pete graciously interrupted. "It's a beautiful day. And besides, you've got the best table at The Tavern."

"I think a beer would be a good idea. Don't you, Hope?" Susan said confidently.

"Yeah, a beer would be a really good idea," replied Hope.

"So what have you t-t-two been talking about?" Jake asked Susan.

"Yeah, our ears were burning all the way back at the house," Cole added.

"Oh, don't flatter yourself, Cole. Your name barely came up," Hope said firmly, yet with a grin.

"Ouch!" Pete said, referring to the tone of Hope's voice. "A chill comes over the campus!"

Cole motioned to a waiter walking by and ordered five beers. Then they all sat down to enjoy the afternoon and hear what the girls had been talking about over lunch.

"Well, I could say it's none of your business and that it was just girl talk. But you guys are my best friends and in this case it actually affects all of us," Hope started in.

"No! You're not leaving school, are you?" shouted Pete.

"No," replied Hope.

"You're bisexual," Pete said jumping back in. "You know, I always thought that about you. I knew it would only be a matter of time. Cole, you are a blessed man!"

"No, Pete, I am not bisexual. I am sorry to disappoint you all," stated Hope. "It's nothing like that."

"What is it, baby?" asked Cole.

"Well, how do I put this?" Hope began. "You guys all know how my mother died when I was young, right?" they all nodded and she continued. "Well, with Susan's help," she said looking at Susan and exchanging smiles, "I've figured out that I have been trying to make up for my mother's absence by trying to take care of my father like she would have, and even trying to take care of all of you guys. So, I have been putting a lot of my own feelings and priorities on hold in order to take care of all of you guys. And I can't do that anymore," she said and gave a big sigh of relief that she had actually gotten it out, especially to Cole.

"Is that it?" Pete asked.

"What do you mean, 'is that it?' I think you are all fortunate she shared it with you, and right away too," Susan said sounding a bit offended by Pete's remark.

"That's n-n-not what he means, Susan," commented Jake. Then looking back at Hope he said, "It's just that we were all wondering when you were going to figure that one out."

"You mean, you knew that?" asked Hope perplexed.

"Well, yeah, it was pretty obvious," Pete answered. "You've been taking such good care of us for so long. We talked about saying something to you, 'cause you know we love ya, Hope. But we figured that there are just some things in life you've got to work through on your own."

"I'll be damned," Susan said, stunned by the well-hidden wisdom of this group of underage beer drinkers. Now it was her turn to be impressed.

"Hey, don't seem so surprised," Jake said boldly. "We're more than just a bunch of pretty faces."

"Not a lot more," Pete said, laughing. "These chiseled features happen to be one of my better qualities," he added, not totally in jest.

As all of this was going on, Cole just sat there smiling as big as anyone could without hurting himself. It was as if he had been unconsciously waiting for this moment as long as he could remember. In the first year and a half of their relationship, he had been completely faithful. It was only in the last year he began to wander into the arms of other women. It was true he had a love for the excitement of the game; but he always had a moment of guilt following his infidelities. He truly wanted to stop. He wanted to be faithful to Hope—he loved her. This had become clear to him even before their romantic hilltop date a few weeks before, when they had dined on lobster and wine and soulful conversation under the magnificent stars.

There had been something in the back of Cole's mind though. Although he couldn't put his finger on it, it hadn't felt right. As he listened to Hope share her thoughts about her mother and what she felt she needed to change, Cole knew this was what hadn't felt right. In the last year, when the guys would talk about Hope's situation, Cole began to take her for granted. He knew she would always forgive him, no matter what he did. As he sat there listening, he knew his unfaithfulness was over for good. Finally everything felt right, and he was so proud of her. Although he had grown and made some better choices for the both of them recently, he realized it was Hope who had held their relationship together all along. And it was Hope who had saved it by becoming the person she was.

"Well, you guys never cease to amaze, do you? And what about you, Mr. Anderson? Did you know too?" Hope said looking at Cole.

Cole leaned forward without saying a word and gave her a huge kiss. "I am so proud of you, baby. Damn! I am proud of you."

Those were usually her words for him. Hope just smiled, taken back by this role reversal. She didn't exactly know what was going on inside his head, but how could she argue with friends who had her best interest at heart. They sat and talked and laughed until the day turned into evening. The sun rolled down over the horizon and the night breeze started to chill the air.

"Cheers!" Susan said as they all raised their glasses in the air.

Hope started in, "To knowing your friends as well as they know themselves."

"And even better," Jake added.

"And even better." They all clinked their mugs together in celebration of themselves.

CHAPTER TEN

"Are you busy, professor?" Cole knocked on Professor McIntry's office door and slowly took a step inside. He noticed a strange feeling as he stepped into the office. It was filled with the same energy that was present during class. It was extremely powerful and he was a little nervous. It wasn't because he was going to talk to a professor; it was that he was talking to a professor he respected. For the first time ever, he felt this was a professor who would actually make a difference in his life.

"Only as busy as I want to be. Come on in, Mr. Anderson. I was just going to have a cup of coffee. Would you care for one?" the professor asked.

"Sure, that would be great," Cole responded.

"Perfect. It's right around the corner. I take mine with just a little cream. Thanks," the professor replied smiling.

Laughing to himself, Cole went around the corner just outside Professor McIntry's office and poured them both a cup of coffee. "With a little cream. Here you go, professor."

Professor McIntry's office was surprisingly neat, something you wouldn't guess from his appearance. It was a simple office, without a lot of the normal workplace clutter. His desk was bare with the exception of a two bins, one marked "in" and the other marked "out," and a couple photos of the professor with friends in different parts of the world. Against the far wall stood two huge bookshelves filled from top to bottom. Cole took a closer look at the pictures and saw one of the professor in front of the Great Pyramids in Egypt and another with his arm around someone who appeared to be Nelson Mandela.

"So how's your spirit today, Cole?" the professor asked.

The professor asked that question the first time he saw anyone, much like other people asked "How are you doing?" or "What's up?" or some other traditional greeting we have come to underappreciate and seldom answer honestly. When the professor asked people that, it made them stop and think. It made them pay attention as they rarely did and honestly give value to their feelings. Of course, people could still lie and say their spirit was fine when it really wasn't; like when someone says "Fine" to the question "How are ya?" purely out of habit—but in reality they weren't even listening to the other person. He was attempting to get people to slow down their lives enough to where they could pay attention to other people. Slow things down enough to where they could start to feel again and not just think their way through their busy little existence.

"Intrigued and confused and happy and a whole bunch of things all at the same time," Cole replied.

"Sounds like your spirit is a bit busy these days. If you keep it running in all those directions, it might get a little tired out," Professor McIntry observed. "Now, to what do I owe the honor of your maiden visit to my office?"

"Ah, I guess I just wanted to talk, you know, about me and things and all these crazy thoughts I've had lately. I mean, if you are too busy I understand."

The professor turned a look on Cole that said, "Come on, you know I am not too busy to help you. Out with it already."

"Well, it's just that I have all these questions," Cole said continuing. "I think about what we talk about in class all the time. Actually, a lot of times I will be talking to my girlfriend, Hope, about something and then we'll discuss it that same week in class. It's like you are answering my questions directly."

"Anything's possible," the professor said quickly. "But let's take one thing at a time. So what kind of questions, Cole?"

"Um…I guess that you probably don't remember what I wrote down as my answer to your 'Who am I?' assignment. So—"

The professor interrupted. "I believe it was something in the nature of…after you wrote everything that described who you were, you actually felt it described more of what you did instead of who you were. So you concluded, to quote you directly, 'I don't have a damn clue who I am!'"

"Yeah, that's right. So why can't I figure out who I am and what I am here to do? I mean, sometimes life just seems so, ah, I don't know, meaningless, I guess. There's got to be more to it, you know?" Cole commented.

"Cole, there are some questions that only you can answer. I can definitely help to guide you along in the process, but nevertheless, it is your journey. Many of your strengths, characteristics, and disciplines are developed while you venture through some of your more challenging and confusing times. Let me say this though, my friend: It is clear you have a fire inside you for learning. Perhaps not learning in the conventional sense as other educators may want, but you have a fire for discovery. For discovering and rediscovering yourself. Trust me when I tell you that your passion will serve you well," the professor added.

"Well, what can I do to make it easier or to get through it faster?" Cole asked. "Is there anything I can do to calm down all this chaos that is going on inside my head to help me focus more?"

"You must remember something very important that will help reduce some of the confusion you are experiencing. You see, Cole, everything in the universe has a natural evolutionary process that it goes through. Whether we're talking about animals, plants or other aspects of nature, stars in the universe, or human beings. All throughout nature things are being born, growing, and developing, and then dying off, only to be regenerated and born again."

The professor looked deeply into Cole's eyes and continued. "What you need to understand is that all the things you are experiencing, all the pains and sufferings, the victories and triumphs, and everything in between, are all part of your own evolutionary process. There is a reason for everything in life. In fact, even death has a reason.

"We definitely have the ability to influence and help shape our life circumstances, but we can't control everything that happens to us. It's crucial to understand, though, that we can certainly control how we react to the things that happen to us. If you live with the knowledge that everything is happening for a reason, you tend to react much differently when you find yourself in a difficult or tense situation. Does that make sense, Cole?"

"So what you are saying is that what is actually happening is not always as important as how we react to what's happening," Cole concluded.

"That's a great way of looking at it. If you think about some of the things that have happened in your past, you can usually figure out some personal benefits for going through that experience. It's just that when you are right in the thick of whatever is happening, it's difficult not to let your emotions get the better of you. How many times have you looked back and wished you dealt with something differently?" Professor McIntry asked.

"Tons of times. Yeah, I hear what you are saying," Cole responded.

"You can certainly plan for the future, Cole, but do your best to keep your attention and focus on the now," added the professor. "Always enjoy the moment you are in, because in reality, it is all there is."

"I don't think I have a problem with that one. Enjoying the moment is my specialty," replied Cole.

"Anyone can enjoy the moment when they are having beers on Saturday night with their friends. It's the more challenging moments that require a little more discipline of thought."

Cole nodded his head in agreement, then Professor McIntry said, "You asked before about things you can do to help increase your focus and control all of the chatter going on inside that head of yours. Are you familiar with meditation?"

"Meditation? Isn't that for those guys who wear orange robes and live in India or something like that?" Cole asked.

Laughing, the professor said, "I think you watch too much TV, Cole. But actually you are partially right. In the past, meditation was something that was only practiced by a small handful of people, most of whom had studied an Eastern or Indian philosophy. It's not the case anymore, as the benefits of meditation have become more widely known throughout the rest of the world. Many people you may view as successful, such as athletes, coaches, and some very wealthy business people, practice meditation daily.

"There are many different forms of meditation, although a pretty widely accepted definition might be as simple as 'deep thought.' I like to see basic meditation as the ability to clear your mind of 'the chaos' as you call it, and refocus it on whatever you choose, while gaining a connection to your true source of power.

"Initially, the benefits may be as simple as being more relaxed, feeling less stress, being able to think more clearly, having more energy, or perhaps sleeping better. But as you continue to practice, you can develop your ability to a point where you can actually begin to co-create the circumstances in your life. All the great thinkers of the world have known this," the professor concluded.

"I want to learn how. Would you be able to teach me, Professor McIntry?" Cole asked.

"Oh, Cole, I don't know. You understand that to be successful at anything takes discipline. Are you sure you are ready?" the professor asked.

"Yeah! I am. I mean, you're not talking about walking on hot coals or sleeping on nails or anything like that, are you?" Cole questioned.

"That's next week's lesson," the professor said laughing. "No, nothing like that. Like I said, we'll start off simple. I'll tell you what. We don't cover this information in class, but if you are willing to commit to one office visit a week, every week, with no exceptions, and practice on your own as well, then we can start."

"Done," Cole said excitedly.

"All right, Cole. Now, in order for you to get any benefit out of the work we will be doing, you must completely trust not only me but also yourself. Just remember that everything is happening for your growth and benefit. So try to let go of any preconceived notions you may have from the past and just enjoy the experience as it happens," Professor McIntry added.

"The first exercise we are going to do is designed so that you can begin to pay attention to your mind and how it works," the professor began. "Sit with your back up against the chair, with your hands resting gently and comfortably in your lap, and your feet flat on the floor. Now close your eyes and take a nice, long, slow, deep breath, breathing in through your nose and out through your mouth. Pay attention to your breathing and feel as if you are filling your body with life. Take another slow, deep breath and as you breathe out, allow yourself to become more and more relaxed. Keep breathing and begin to feel yourself relaxing from the top of your head, down through your shoulders, and through the rest of your body, and down through your legs, and feel your entire body completely relaxed and calm," McIntry continued. "As you sit there relaxed and completely aware, pay attention to your thoughts as they come in and out of your mind. For the next five minutes, just sit and continue to breathe and pay attention to your thoughts."

Cole sat in the chair, following the professor's instructions and his mind began to race. He started thinking about the professor and how well he actually knew him. Should he be allowing the professor to do this to him. This was all so new, so different. What was going on? What the hell was the professor doing? Was he hypnotizing him or putting him under some kind of spell? Was he going to bark like a dog every time he heard a bell ring or something like that? No, that wasn't possible. The professor was apparently a few cards short of a full deck, but his intentions were good, weren't they? Besides, he had been teaching at the University for years, so he couldn't very well have been turning unsuspecting students into zombies through some meditative voodoo practice. Could he? "No, that's ridiculous," Cole thought to himself. But as he took another deep breath, he started to relax and realize he did trust Professor McIntry. He knew the professor wouldn't do anything that would hurt him. Cole knew he had so many questions and he wanted some answers. He wanted to figure some things out.

Cole's thoughts continued to race in every direction imaginable. Five minutes he had to sit there, just thinking? It already seemed like an hour had passed by. He wondered what the professor was doing right now. Was he sitting there staring at Cole? Was he out getting another cup of coffee? Was he writing down psychological notes about Cole's every movement or eye twitch? Perhaps it wasn't Professor McIntry who had lost touch with reality. Maybe it was the professor who had the "real" grasp on reality and everyone else was a few cards short of a full deck. Maybe he could see things differently, and the rest just hadn't caught up to him yet. It was possible, wasn't it?

"Now I want you to still your mind," the professor spoke softly. "I want you to clear your mind of all thoughts and images and simply let it become calm, quiet, and clear."

"Clear my mind? That's absurd," thought Cole. How in the world would he clear his mind, when there were always thoughts of some kind going on up there? He gathered his focus and began to try. "Okay, just think about nothing," he said to himself. As quickly as he said it, in popped an image of Hope, then of Jake, ah...it was useless. Thoughts rolled through his imagination even more quickly than before. "I can't believe I can't do this," he thought. "Why can't I just relax?" His emotions started to build, as he became frustrated at not being able to get a hold on his thoughts.

"Okay, Cole, when you are ready, open your eyes," the professor said.

"I don't think I quite got it, professor," commented Cole, feeling a bit disappointed.

"You experienced exactly what you were supposed to," McIntry replied. "As far as being able to control the direction of your thoughts, trust me, it simply takes practice. For now, why don't you tell me what was happening when you tried to clear your mind."

"It was like my brain went into overdrive. I tried to think about nothing, and then nothing reminded me of something, and then something reminded me of something else. It was crazy! I mean, how the hell do you think about nothing?" Cole complained.

Laughing, the professor said, "It's all right, Cole, really. Be patient. I told you this wasn't an overnight process. I want you to do exactly what we just did today everyday for at least five minutes. Pay attention to your thoughts and remember to keep your breathing slow, deep, and relaxed. To help you clear your mind, try focusing in on a small dot of light, perhaps white or yellow, way out in the distance of your imagination. This will allow you to clear the thoughts from your mind, but will give you something tangible to focus on so that your rational mind will have something to do. Each day, increase the time you spend focusing in on that dot of light," he concluded. "Any questions, Cole?"

"Yeah, plenty. But I think we can save them for another time. I really want to thank you. I appreciate the extra time, professor," Cole said sincerely.

"It is my pleasure, Cole. Who knows, you may even be one of those exceptional students I talked about in class," the professor added as Cole was turning to walk out the door.

Cole turned briefly, looked at the professor's half-cocked smiling face, then walked out of his office. "What the hell just happened?" he thought to himself. "What did I just do?" Although he wasn't sure what exactly just happened, something about it felt right. He walked outside into the bright sunshine. Looking at his watch, he realized that although it seemed like he had been with the professor for hours and hours, it had only been about thirty minutes. Coming out of the ether of the professor's office, Cole looked up into the cloudless sky and realized that he had an important decision at hand: Go to biology or get something to eat. He went to lunch.

CHAPTER ELEVEN

The next few weeks seemed to slip by as if each day were a single grain of sand falling through the thin stem of an hourglass, barely noticed until many of them had already passed. So much was happening among the little gang at SCSU. As spring approached their busy campus and busier lives, the group of friends found themselves on new ground. It's an interesting feeling to be in uncharted waters. There is a power that comes when forging ahead toward somewhere you have never been or something you have never done. As the flowers started to bloom around the campus, they explored this new, unknown territory.

Pete's baseball season was in high gear, and Coach Numbnuts' decision to start him proved to be a good one as Pete's achievements on the field continued to stand out. Although Pete was doing well on the surface, he began to feel a little isolated within the group. Everyone else was on an inner journey in one way or another, but he just continued with business as usual.

That in itself was fine by Pete; he didn't get what all the commotion was about anyway. Searching for inner feelings, thinking about a life's purpose, and exploring your repressed emotions weren't things that Pete did often. In fact, the way he saw it, if you look too deeply into yourself, you're bound to find something you don't like, and that just screws with your mind, causing all kinds of unwanted thoughts. He said the major benefit of being shallow was nothing really bothered you that wasn't actually happening right then.

Pete was brilliantly light-hearted in that way, and he could always be counted on to insist on doing something that was fun, required energy, and made you feel good. Although he wasn't a guy you'd want on your team of scientists looking to discover a new galaxy, he'd be the first one to call if you wanted to have a fun night out, regardless of the circumstances.

Jake and Susan were seeing more of each other and developing a nice relationship. They understood each other and had a tremendous communication between them. Little by little, as Jake began to feel more comfortable with Susan, his stutter became less severe when talking with her. When around new women for the first time, he still managed to sound like a machine gun, spitting out words in small inconsistent bursts. But since he wasn't trying to impress them, he really didn't care how he sounded. They started working on the possible causes of his stuttering and figured it had something to do with how poorly his parents had treated him. But Jake decided to tackle that psychoanalysis at a later time.

Both of them had found something in each other that neither one of them had experienced before. Jake had found a young woman with independence, strength, a great sense of herself and her direction, and a love for helping others. With Susan, Jake could be himself, really himself. And Susan had found a young man who was growing every day, a man with inner strength and outer gentleness. In a world that has become more advanced in technology than in its sense of humanity, Jake's humanistic glow shone admirably. He was the proverbial "nice guy" growing into an even nicer man. It took someone like Susan to understand how valuable those qualities were in a relationship and pierce the bitter irony of Jake's loneliness.

Hope continued to explore her new understanding of herself and the emotions she had suppressed for so long. Alongside this exploration and discovery came the new confidence she had longed for. For the first time in years, she had a new identity. She was no longer just Clayton Stewart's daughter or Cole Anderson's girlfriend; she had become Hope Stewart.

In shaking free from the mother role, she had been able to develop parts of her personality she never could before. Hope and Cole began to talk often about their personal transformations. In many ways it was Cole's questioning of himself and his purpose in life that allowed Hope to break away from her own past. Cole's desire to learn more about who he was and what life was all about had influenced Hope to really start looking at herself.

Cole continued to practice the meditations and visualizations he learned in his private sessions with the professor. As he began to gain better control over his thoughts and his mind, he started thinking more clearly and feeling much more energetic.

As Cole and Hope's individual journeys began to develop, they often talked about how unique it was that their connection to each other had grown deeper and stronger. They had heard so many people talk about the need to be "committed to a relationship" and give up part of themselves to make it work. They had always had a bond and a desire to be together, but now they also had developed trust and a better understanding of themselves. They could communicate on a completely different level than before. Their commitment now wasn't "to the relationship" but more to a mutual respect. This understanding allowed them to continue on intertwining paths. They no longer *needed* to be with each other; they simply *wanted* to be with each other.

The group got together often, sometimes just the two couples, sometimes with Pete, and sometimes Pete brought along his female of choice for the evening. They sat around talking endlessly about everything. Hope, Cole, and Jake talked a lot about the discussions from Professor McIntry's class.

Although Susan had already taken the class, she still loved to explore the information with others. Besides, the professor's lessons were a little different every semester. In class, they had discussed things like great spiritual revolutions and political uprisings, like China's Tiananmen Square. They had talked about the need for an understanding of self before there could be an understanding of others.

They had completed the sentence "Happiness is…" and heard every possible answer you could think of. People's ideas of what happiness was varied from "good friends" to "being loved" to "good sex" to "a cold beer and a video game." The professor combined lessons of laughter with wisdom and blended spiritual insight with realism. He combined lessons from great historical figures wonderfully with practical applications that could be used to create better results today. Professor McIntry began to weave a magical tapestry of possibility into their lives. The class quickly became the highlight of their week. And Cole's private visits to the professor's office, which he kept strictly to himself, became the sessions he looked forward to the most.

Each of them, in their own way, had developed a passion for the mystery of things, except possibly for Pete who often just nodded in agreement or got bored and found something entertaining to do. They talked about the collective power of young people and how none of them could relate to the world their parents lived in: Work really hard at something you don't like and don't believe in. For what? A few bucks? To this somewhat enlightened group it just didn't make sense.

"Yeah, I don't really get it either," Cole responded to Hope's question. They were sitting around the house one night engulfed in conversation, enlivened by the sounds of Dave Matthews playing in the background and adding empties to the bottles of beer that covered the coffee table. "How the hell could you work at a job for thirty years that you weren't happy with, just to pay some bills? It just seems so pointless. I mean, if you're not happy, what's the use?"

"I know what you mean," Susan was quick to agree. "You hear so many people say they have developed a certain lifestyle and they need a certain amount of money to sustain it, so they're stuck in their job." Susan continued, "As for me, I think I'd rather be happy and enjoy what I am doing all along the way, even if I don't make as much money, instead of putting it off until my life is half over just so I can have a little extra 'stuff.' All that material stuff doesn't make you happy anyway. Sure, it's fun to play with and nice to look at, but I think it's the people in your life that fill you up with happiness, don't you think?"

"But why can't you have all of it?" Cole asked. "I mean, can't you do something you enjoy, make a lot of money, and have people around who care about you and who you care about?"

"Absolutely!" exclaimed Pete out of nowhere. They all looked at him, surprised he was even listening. "Yeah, I know. You guys don't think I pay attention to you when you start talking about all this philosophical stuff. Well, the truth is that most of the time I don't. But the Padres are up by six in the bottom of the eighth and the game is pretty much wrapped up. So I guess my attention wandered from what's normally important to me, which is my cold beverage and the baseball game, and has moved over to you guys.

"If you ask me, all I need is a job that is somehow sports-related, a hot-looking wife who loves me and loves sex, enough cash to keep us in a decent house, a sports utility vehicle that can fit the dog in the back, beers and food in the fridge, and a small handful of people I can call friends and can trust with my life. Give me some simple pleasures and you couldn't stop me from smiling. Hell, if they started paying me to play ball and you subtracted school, I've got exactly that right now, minus the dog. I wouldn't change a thing!"

For all of Pete's crudeness and his simplistic view of the world, there was a beautifully pointed wisdom in what he said. Hope, Cole, Susan, and Jake looked at each other as Pete took a big swig of beer and faded back into the baseball game as quickly as he had come into their conversation. Was Pete on to something here? Had he figured it out before anyone else? They contemplated Pete's simple formula, each of them assessing how their own version of happiness would fit into it.

After their thoughts and conversation had switched to something more basic like what movie they were going to see this weekend, and they had enjoyed a few more beers, it was getting late. Hope and Cole decided to call it a night and went into Cole's room to go to sleep. Susan ended up staying over that night and Pete made a few late night phone calls so that he wouldn't have to go to bed alone.

Pete had that ability. He could always find someone to come over, to go on a date with, or even just to hang out. It was interesting, because most people saw him as some kind of a jerk because he was always dating more than one girl at a time.

For as long as they all had known each other, Pete had at least two girlfriends all the time. The interesting part was that Pete told them all about each other. For some reason, they didn't seem to care. They enjoyed his company enough to look past the fact that they weren't the only person he spent time with. He even came clean about whatever original story he had come up with to pick them up in the first place. Ironically enough, most of them just laughed. He was beautifully simple and the women he attracted loved him for it.

"Ahhhh!" Cole shouted and sat up quickly as if jumping right out of his dream and waking up Hope in the process.

"What is it, honey? Are you all right?" Hope asked with some concern.

"Yeah, yeah, I'm fine. It was just a dream," Cole said, regaining his senses. But he'd been scared. He was sweating all over and his heart was racing a mile a minute. "But damn, it seemed so real, Hopes. It was all so real," he added.

"Do you want to tell me about it?" she asked.

"No, it's okay. Let's just go back to sleep." That was Cole's answer, but it wasn't what he felt. How could he tell someone about a dream that didn't make any sense?

Besides, it was just a dream and it wasn't real. It looked and felt real, but it was just in his imagination. As he thought that to himself, he remembered the professor's words that first day in class: "Your mind doesn't know the difference." Those words shook him. He started thinking back over the events of his dream, trying to remember every little detail...

Hope and Cole were walking through an open field, holding hands, and taking in the stars as they would on a clear night. The grass was thick and plush and felt almost alive under their feet. A light on a house behind them illuminated a clear path where they walked. There was just the tiniest sliver of a moon, which allowed the light of the stars to shine brightly. Something was bothering both of them, but he couldn't remember what it was. They looked into each other's eyes, but their feelings of love were interrupted by this haunting feeling, and they were disturbingly unaware of its cause.

As they walked and took in the calming effects of Cole's millions of little therapists in the sky, a beautiful butterfly hovered gently in the air around them. It was brilliant in color. Full deep shades of green, orange, red, and yellow gave this lovely creature a magnificent quality. They stopped and watched it dance around in the sky above their heads, then bounce down and wave to them right in front of their faces. The butterfly flipped and landed delicately on Hope's shoulder.

Watching it perched there lightly, one of God's beautiful creations resting on another of God's beautiful creations, Cole started to think about how this butterfly came to be, how it had started out as this feeble caterpillar just months or maybe even days ago. He thought about how this seemingly useless little worm, with no apparent talent or beauty, had transformed itself into the incredible image he saw before him. "What an amazing feat of nature," he thought. And he said to Hope, "I wonder how many people are caterpillars that just haven't transformed yet. I wonder how many people have this kind of magical beauty lying dormant within them and it just hasn't had a chance to take life. I mean, if you look at a little caterpillar, you can't tell it is going to turn out like this. It just looks like a hairy worm."

"You're right," replied Hope. "It makes you wonder how many people would turn into butterflies given the right circumstances, or influences, or opportunity."

Just as she was finishing her sentence, there was a huge noise in the distance beyond the hill in front of them. It was a deafeningly loud crash of some sort. They couldn't see what it was, but they felt the impact right through to their bones. As they went to take a step toward the direction of the crash, the beautiful butterfly lifted off of Hope's shoulder and turned into a huge, black buzzard right in front of their eyes. It was cawing and screeching and trying to claw at their faces. It was enormous, with a four-foot wingspan. It hovered there flapping its wings and just as it was about to sink its razor sharp claws into Hope—

Cole awoke. It had all seemed so real. But what did it mean? What was the butterfly about? Or the crash? Or the buzzard? Was it just a dream that meant nothing at all or did it have some symbolic message for him to take note of? Whatever it was, he wouldn't forget it. He stared at the ceiling while Hope slept peacefully beside him, unaware of the perils she had just faced in his dreamtime. He wasn't frightened but preoccupied, and he couldn't get the images out of his mind. He finally fell asleep and awoke late next morning, deciding not to tell anyone the details of his horrific "experience" of the past night.

CHAPTER TWELVE

"Greetings, my fellow journeymen. How are your spirits today?" boomed the professor as he walked into the auditorium in his usual flip-flops and Hawaiian shirt.

"Hung over!" yelled someone from the back of the room, and the entire class laughed heartily.

"Ah yes, the painstaking aftermath of overconsumption, and indeed a tragedy for you, my friend. Let us all please take a moment of silence to recognize the agony this young man must be enduring." The professor's sarcasm was interrupted by more laughter. "Nevertheless, even in the midst of unfortunate circumstances we can find a lesson and, ironically, our tired and sickly friend here has given us a perfect illustration for our lesson today…cause and effect.

"We have all heard one of Sir Isaac Newton's Laws of Motion, which states 'for every action there is an equal and opposite reaction,' right?" Shouts of confirmation echoed through the hall and the professor resumed. "That statement is usually used to describe energy in chemistry or physics class, but I want to take it into your everyday life and describe it in terms of the effects your everyday choices have on your life. I want everyone to listen very carefully. This is an easy lesson to listen to, but often a difficult one to actually hear. Very similar to how most of you live your lives. Things happen, but you don't really pay attention to what it is that is happening. I've said it once and I'll say it again: Life gives you so much pleasure, joy, comical irony, and mystery, if you simply just pay attention," the professor bellowed. He took a step back as if in deep thought and continued. "Back to cause and effect. Every single thought you think has an effect on the rest of the universe."

At this statement, some of the class laughed, some looked at him in disbelief and others sat on the edge of their seats waiting for what he was going to say next.

"Thought is the predecessor to any action. Can we agree on that?" asked the professor. "Everyone here can at least agree that an action cannot take place until a thought occurs. It's pretty clear you have to think it, whether consciously or subconsciously, before you can actually do something, right?" Everyone nodded. "All right, so let me take things a step further. Could we agree that your originating thought puts into motion a series of events, or in other words, a series of causes, which create effects, which create more causes, which create more effects?"

"One more time, professor," requested a student from the front of the class. "You kind of lost me on that last part."

"All right. Let's say, for example, you thought about skipping a class one day."

"I think about that everyday," shouted someone and laughter disrupted the class.

"Thank you for that, Mr. Barely Passing. We all appreciate your insight. Ah, there are so many lost souls, my friends. We are going to need a bigger flashlight!" said the professor and a coy smile spread across his bearded face. "Okay, so you think about skipping a class," he continued. "That is your originating thought. You make the choice, based on that thought, not to go to class. So your thought was the cause, and missing class was the effect, right?" The class nodded, showing they were following him so far.

"So let's say during that class you skipped, the professor reviewed an important piece of information that would count for thirty percent of your grade on the final. You weren't there to learn it, so you ended up failing the final. Failing the final causes your overall grade point average to drop below satisfactory and you get put on academic probation. You can't play football on academic probation, and you were a star player. The season doesn't go nearly as well as it would have and your team doesn't go to a bowl game. That means a loss of revenue to the school and less exposure for the team and key players who were looking to go to the pros." The professor paused, then asked, "Do you see how that entire chain of events is linked back to your original thought of skipping class?"

"Yeah, professor. But isn't that exaggerating things a little?" a student asked.

"Is it really?" Professor McIntry replied. "Are you saying what I just described isn't a possibility? Wake up my friends! This happens every day. It happens to *you* every day in your life.

"Hey, by now you all know that I would be the first person to say you need humor in life and that most people take things way too seriously. But there is a big difference between joking around and being a joke. In order to have fun playing the game, you must understand how the game works, otherwise joking around quickly becomes a mask for not knowing what the hell is going on." He looked into the crowd knowing that last statement would hit some people hard. "I lived under that mask for a long time, my friends, a very long time. It's up to you if you want to remove yours." He took a pause, seeing that he had really gotten the students' wheels turning.

"What is your life if not a series of interrelated events? Aren't all these events shaped by the thoughts you think, which cause you to make the choices you do? And are the thoughts you think not influenced by your past experiences? You see, my friends, it is all interwoven. It's an incredibly brilliant pattern, and each and every moment has the capacity to change the direction of everything that is yet to come."

"Well, what about fate?" asked a student from the back. "What about the idea that the events in your life are predetermined in some way? You know, like destiny?"

"What do the rest of you think about that question?" The professor addressed the class.

"I believe in fate," said a girl in the front row. "I think there are some things you are destined to have or do in your life. Like finding a soul mate," she said, smiling.

"I don't know about that," commented Cole. "I think you make your life what you choose."

"Would you like to elaborate on that, Mr. Anderson?" asked Professor McIntry.

"Well," continued Cole, "I don't know. I don't really see how fate or some magical force is going to take you somewhere regardless of what you do. That's like saying you have no control over your life and your choices don't matter. I'd like to think you can do whatever you want to do in life, and that you choose your own destiny."

"Very good, both of you," suggested the professor. "Who else has a comment on this?"

Hope stepped in and asked, "From what you were just explaining to us about cause and effect, are you saying all the things that happen to us in our life are determined by what we think?"

"Friends, what I can offer you is my opinion on how this works. It does happen that my opinion is backed up by information supported by science and physics as well as nearly every philosophy and religion in the world, nevertheless it's still an opinion." The professor waited for the chuckles to quiet down before continuing. "I feel we all create our circumstances moment by moment with the thoughts we think and the feelings we have, which result in the choices we make. Most people understand this on a basic level. They realize they need to think positively and have a good attitude in order for things to work out the way they want them to. Everyone, for the most part, wants to be happy. They want to enjoy pleasant circumstances and experience success in life's arenas, whether simple or difficult. Although people say they want this or that, unfortunately most people don't really believe they can accomplish it. Instead of their inner thoughts and feelings being secure in belief and confidence and filled with positive expectation, most people's inner thoughts are insecure and filled with fear and lack of confidence.

"You must make a commitment to yourself to direct your thoughts, feelings, and speech to support what you desire to happen. How many times do you talk about the things you actually don't want to happen?" the professor asked, already knowing the answer. "Think about it. How often do you say things like 'I hope I don't fail this test' or 'I better not get caught' or 'I don't want to fall asleep' when you are actually trying to stay awake?" The class nodded in agreement. "We make efforts to get what we want, but we talk about what we don't want. That is one of the quickest paths to failure and frustration. You are creating a self-fulfilling prophecy, and you will be sure to get what you ask for.

"To give you another example, I play golf every chance I get and I think it is such a beautiful metaphor for life. I've just got to laugh when I am playing with someone who switches to an old ball when they are hitting over water, just in case they hit it in, so they won't be upset if they lose a good, brand new ball. Now what kind of message is that person sending to his subconscious mind? One that spells confidence or one that spells disaster?"

"Disaster," the students all said.

"Exactly. That person is saying to himself, 'Well, there is this big lake here, and I usually hit it right in the middle, and I don't really believe that this time is going to be any different than before.' My friends, if you are going to hit the shot with a thought process like that, save yourself the trouble and the aggravation, and just skip the hole altogether. When you are hitting over a lake," continued Professor McIntry, "my suggestion would be to pick out the most expensive ball you can find and take a whack at it like you're a pro. Instead of thinking you are some hack who is about to make his ball do a swan dive into the lake, imagine yourself to be Tiger Woods and that this shot is to win the PGA Championship or U.S. Open. Think and visualize and desire the outcome you want to occur. Think of nothing else other than the outcome you desire, and believe it to be already accomplished." He paused, then asked, "how many times do you find yourself with a lake, or some other major obstacle, in front of you in your life? Move through it with confidence and be careful to think only about the outcome you desire.

"I can't emphasize this enough, my fellow journeymen. Your thoughts are very powerful. Indeed, they are. They are the tools by which you construct your life. Whether you continually hit the ball into the lake or onto the green is completely up to you and the quality of your thinking.

"I'd like to revisit our question on destiny versus personal choice and ask you to explore something. By a show of hands, who believes in fate or destiny, or that there is something you are chosen to do or be in life?" About a third of the class raised their hands. "And who feels that it is up to you to choose your destiny?" The rest of the hands went up. "Could it be a combination of both forces working? In other words, could you have a predetermined fate or destiny, but it's up to you to make the choices and decisions in your life in order to find it?"

The class nodded, liking this last thought.

"How do you know when you've done something right or when you've made the choice that is right for you?" Professor McIntry asked. "Now before you answer, it's important to understand when I say 'right for you' I am not referring to right or wrong in the sense that most people view it. Right or wrong implies judgment, and judgment never leads anyone to the place they wish to go. There is no right or wrong in our world, there just is. Just ask Winnie the Pooh; he is one of the greatest Taoist in history." The professor quickly asked another question before the class could catch up with his serious but comical example.

"Okay, so how do you know when you've made a choice that is supportive of your journey?" he asked again.

"When it feels right," Hope commented, shouting out.

"Yeah, I think you can just tell," another student started in. "When I make a decision that isn't the best, it's almost like my body tells me it wasn't right."

"And when you make a tough decision, or one that isn't supportive of you, where do you usually feel it?" the professor asked.

A number of shouts came out from the class, implying that most people had at least had the experience before. "In the pit of my stomach," they said.

"Exactly. There is a lot of truth to what was said just a minute ago: Your body tells you whether you've made a decision that supports who you are. It's unfortunate most people don't pay attention to their bodies. We see people continue to do things even though their body is physically telling them to stop. And we see these people develop ulcers, recurring migraines, and other illnesses. My belief is that your body can physically feel the expression of your emotions and feelings.

"The area you are referring to as the 'pit of your stomach' is what's called your solar plexus. The solar plexus is a mass of nerves that, on a medical chart, you would literally find 'in the pit of your stomach,' or right behind it anyway. Basically, this area is believed to be where you integrate your right- and left-brain functions or in other words, it's where your intellectual thoughts meet your emotional expressions. So when you make a decision that doesn't support who you are, it's as if the emotional you is disagreeing with the intellectual you and causing a disturbance or pain in the place in your body where those two systems meet," the professor explained.

"Professor," Jake chimed in, "what you just said was that our thinking and feeling can actually cause a sensation in our body. Are you also saying then, that we can cure or improve a physical pain or disease by working with our thoughts and emotions?"

"That's a great question," replied the professor. "Before I give you my answer, I want to know how you all feel about that?"

"Are you talking about curing cancer or something by waving your hands over someone and shouting some voodoo gibberish, like they do in Haiti or something?" asked one of the students. "That stuff isn't real or anything, is it?"

"There are many people who believe it is very real. Remember, everyone, what is 'real' for one," the professor continued, gesturing quotation marks around the word real, "may not be real for another. Something is real for a person when they believe it to be real for them. Keep in mind our reality is very subjective; it is what we want it to be." He paused, then said, "But that's not exactly what I'm talking about, and I think the question was referring to things a bit more mainstream.

"Is there anyone who is not familiar with the term psychosomatic? Basically, it is when an illness is either brought on or made worse by a person's emotional state." The professor waited to see if any hands went up. "Okay, so we can at least all agree there is some validity to that, right? There are many everyday examples we can probably all agree on, such as a person getting hypertension or an ulcer from being overly stressed or someone getting an upset stomach when they are nervous. There are many people who feel the majority of all illness or disease is caused by your thoughts and feelings.

"I find it very interesting that most people can see very clearly how your emotions may cause you to have a headache, but they wouldn't even consider that your emotional state could self-induce a more serious condition like cancer." He looked to see if most people were following his train of thought. "Now, it would make perfect sense that, if someone's out-of-balance emotional makeup caused a particular illness, that re-balancing their emotional makeup would go a long way toward curing it. Correct?"

"Are you saying that someone can cure cancer with their thoughts?" asked a disbelieving student.

"What I am saying," Professor McIntry continued, "is that I believe it is definitely possible. Let's take a look at the actual word 'disease.' We can break it down to 'dis' and 'ease.' 'Dis' means 'separation from' and 'ease' means 'freedom from pain or comfort.' So having a disease literally means 'to be separated from your freedom from pain.' In other words, 'not being free of pain.'

"Now, I am certainly not an expert on holistic healing and I am not a medical doctor, so all I can offer is my own experience. The question I want you to think about is this. I want you to remember back to the first day of class. Why is it so simple for you to understand that when you focus your thoughts on something as simple as eating an apple, you can cause your glands to produce saliva? But then you have such a hard time believing your thoughts can influence the other organs of your body?

"Your thoughts and emotions cause your glands to release adrenalin when you're excited or scared," he continued, "causing your heart rate to speed up, or when you are asleep or deeply relaxed your heart slows down. But these are temporary effects and are influenced by the thought or emotion we are currently experiencing. Worry and stress can cause a myriad of different physical ailments, which are widely accepted as psychosomatic. We have all heard different stories of people who have defied all of the doctor's predictions and conclusions and have literally 'willed' themselves back toward good health. When you look at the human body, it is created and built to continually replenish the old, used and no longer productive parts with new, working and healthy ones. Dead skin flakes off as healthy skin takes its place. Old cells die off as new ones are replenished every day. These regenerative processes of our body are ongoing, and are automatic. They are controlled by our subconscious, just like our breathing or our circulation.

"What I want you to explore, because you need to come to your own conclusions and beliefs about this, is why those functions, which are always performed automatically and carried out with perfection over and over again, would cease to work as they always have. Why would your immune system let a tumor develop in your body instead of fighting off the disease like it would any other independent infection or abnormality? Could it be that you have created something, perhaps by your thoughts or emotions, that is blocking or preventing your system from working properly?" The professor paused, knowing the class was now starting to open up to different possibilities.

"I want you to explore this and continue to think about it, and do some outside research. I don't want you to automatically take my opinion. Hell, I'm just some whacked-out professor who doesn't even wear real shoes," he said, breaking the tension of heavy thought. "If you accept what I say in this class as ultimate fact, without researching it on your own, it's no different from buying into the *status quo* just because that is the prevailing opinion.

"I want you to develop independent thinking, and be able to create true freedom of thought and expression. Only then will you be able to call yourself an individual. Only then will you be truly happy with yourself. Why? Because you independently developed your own truth. That's why. You didn't automatically take on your parents' truth, or society's truth, or the government's truth, or even my truth. You created your own. You created your *self*. Now, does that mean you will disagree with how your parents raised you or what society pumped out as fact? Well, not necessarily. What it means is you will understand clearly *why* you believe what you believe. That creates strength of character and promotes harmony among your thoughts, emotions, feelings and actions…and that, my friends, spells out a happy and fulfilling life. So, all of my young, passionate, little journeymen, let's keep working on finding 'your' truth. See you next week."

CHAPTER THIRTEEN

"Let's do something different tonight," said Cole. It was Thursday evening happy hour and the gang was at his house this week, lounging around the living room listening to music. The earliest any of them had class on Friday was eleven o'clock, and Pete didn't have class on Friday at all. So on Thursdays, they ritualistically celebrated the coming of the weekend with a few beverages. Tonight there were nothing but happy couples: Cole and Hope, Jake and Susan...and Pete had asked Debra, the girl from the taco stand with whom he hung out from time to time.

"So you want different. How about we drink Bud Light instead of Miller Lite?" Pete suggested with a chuckle.

"No, seriously, different sounds good," said Jake. "We haven't been down to the beach in a while."

"Why don't we bring some food and drinks and blankets and do the whole bonfire thing?" suggested Hope.

"That sounds great," replied Susan.

"All right, it's a plan. Everybody in?" asked Cole looking for a last confirmation.

Everyone agreed and they started getting things together for their excursion. The campus wasn't far from the beach, but too far to walk with all the stuff they were going to bring. Pete, Debra, Susan, and Hope decided they would load up Susan's car with the cooler and blankets, and go to the store for food. They would meet Jake and Cole at the beach, after the guys picked up some wooden pallets for the bonfire. They figured they would drop the cars off at the house and walk back down to the beach, so they could all enjoy a good buzz without being concerned about driving home.

"Let's get down there for the sunset if we can," said Hope as everyone scurried to help fill the cooler and load up the car.

"All right. We'll meet you down there in about a half hour, then Jake and I will drop the cars off," Cole said and they hopped in the Jeep and sped off.

"Ahhhhhhhhhhhhhh, slow down Cole!" screamed Jake from his perch on top of Cole's handlebars. They had decided the bike would be faster than walking back to the beach. Jake was grabbing on for dear life as Cole raced down the street ignoring his pleas. "Stop before we get to the sand or I'm gonna get frickin' drilled!"

"Sure thing, buddy," replied Cole as he sped up. This was one of those unwritten rules of long-time friends: If you had an opportunity to put a good friend in an awkward situation, and you knew he wouldn't get seriously hurt, then you were obligated by an inexplicable, spiritual force to take full advantage of that opportunity. The obligation was heightened if there was water, mud, or women involved in some way. In this case, it was just pure fun. Cole raced toward the sand with Jake propped up uncomfortably on the handlebars, screaming and shouting the entire time.

"Here we go!" yelled Cole. And Jake prepared to abandon ship when he realized Cole wasn't planning to stop.

"Cole, you son of a biiiiiiiittttch!" exclaimed Jake as the bike hit the sand, knocked him out of his crouch and sent him flying forward. He hit the ground with a thud and tumbled three or four times before coming to a stop. "You little bastard!" Jake exclaimed, shaking sand out of his hair.

"The landing was a bit weak, I'll give you an eight point five!" Pete called from the sidelines.

"Yeah, you're a million laughs, Pete. Ladies, do you see the kind of friends I have here? They're the best, aren't they?" Jake said with a half-smirk on his face. He wasn't really mad. He understood the unwritten rule as well as any of them. He just wanted to get a little harmless bitching in while he could.

They settled down and gathered around the fire pit. Pete and Cole stacked up the wooden pallets so the bonfire would be ready to light once the sun went down. The women got out the sandwiches and salads. Jake made himself a little mound of sand to lean up against while he watched them work. He sat in his sand recliner and cracked the first beer of the evening. "Ah, nothing like a cold beer after being thrown off a bike," he said sarcastically and everyone laughed.

As they ate and drank, the sun began to set on the horizon of the Pacific Ocean. The skyline was magnificent that evening. The sun glowed a vibrant orange and sank slowly into what seemed like the next world, past the edge of the glistening waters. Colors lit up the sky, reflecting off soft clouds that stretched across the sun.

"That's so beautiful," commented Debra. "I just love sunsets."

"Yeah, it's pretty incredible. Look how the clouds come across the sun like that and take the colors up into the sky," Cole added. "It's just amazing. Hey, guys, do you remember the sunset on number eighteen that day?"

"Who could forget that?" Pete replied with Jake nodding in agreement.

"What was the sunset at eighteen?" Susan asked.

"Well, one afternoon my father and the three of us were out playing golf," Cole began. "It was a fantastic day, although I think we were hacking up the course pretty badly."

"Speak for yourself," interrupted Pete.

"Anyway," Cole continued, "so we were on about hole sixteen or so when we noticed the incredible sunset. It was one of those sunsets that had just the perfect amount of clouds in the sky, where the sun lights them up brilliantly but doesn't drown them out. The colors shot high into the sky, the reds and oranges, yellows and purples…. It was awesome and we all noticed it. It spread out far across the sky and made it about halfway around the horizon. It was unique because usually a sunset only glows right where the sun goes down, but this one seemed to stretch out forever. And it gets better.

"We all hit our second shots off the eighteenth fairway and we came up toward the green. As we parked the carts and walked onto the green, and I was waiting for my turn to putt, I looked up into the sky and I couldn't believe it. I got everyone's attention and told them to look up. It was spectacular. The sunset completely encircled the horizon. It was a full three-hundred-and-sixty- degree sunset. None of us had ever seen anything like it before and none of us has since. It was bright red and orange right where the sun was hitting the horizon, but the low wispy clouds stretched the colors all the way around until they surrounded us. We stood there looking, turning slowly in circles, taking it all in, not fully believing what we were seeing." Cole took a breath. "You know, that was one of my great moments. It was perfect. I mean, think about it. Just think about the sense of perfect timing Mother Nature had in providing us with that incredible vision. If we'd teed off fifteen minutes earlier or taken an extra ten minutes looking for a lost ball, or anything else, it would have thrown off the timing. We wouldn't have seen that most beautiful end to the day at the same time that we finished our golf game."

"I think about that day every time there's an incredible sunset, like tonight," commented Jake.

"Yeah, that really was something," said Pete, "even your Pops saw the poetry in it. I remember him telling your mom when we got back."

"I once heard a wise man say that life is a pretty incredible experience if you just pay attention," Hope mused and everyone, with the possible exception of Debra, knew she was referring to Professor McIntry.

"It sure is, but I also think it depends on what eyes you're looking through," said Susan.

"Huh?" said Pete.

"What do you mean, Susan?" asked Jake.

"What I mean is everyone is different. We all have different backgrounds and experiences, beliefs and ideas, fears and strengths. Sure, the six of us have some similarities in some of those areas, which is probably what has drawn us to be friends. But for the most part, people look at things so differently," answered Susan. "I think the way you view life makes a big difference on the kinds of experiences you actually have. Some people think life is so difficult and they have been dealt an unfair hand, and those people usually lead pretty challenging lives. Other people view the world as abundant and a place to be creative and grow, and life usually is pretty simple for them. Not always easy, but it's usually pretty simple." She stopped for a moment then said, "Like the wise man you talked about says, 'Your perception is your reality.' Beautiful sunset or L.A. smog, I guess it's all up to us."

"I think sometimes our eyes could use a little compassion, a sense of humor and a lot less judgment," concluded Jake.

They sat peacefully, respecting the beauty around them, not just the sunset, but the true beauty of their cherished friendships as well. As the final arc of sun sank into the world beyond the horizon, Pete entertained them with animated stories from baseball practice. Pete was just as funny to watch as to listen to. His arms flailed about with enthusiasm and he'd usually change his voice to fit whoever he was talking about. He liked to make people smile, and he loved to make them laugh.

Sometimes there is nothing like a good laugh to set your spirit free. Laughter is medicine for the soul. It heals old wounds and creates new joys. It's hard to dislike someone who makes you laugh; it's a quality appreciated by everyone. It's amazing how laughter can give a person amnesia about the problems they thought were so monumental. There are a lot of things someone can live without, but laughter isn't one of them.

"Come on, boys. Let's get that fire lit," requested Hope in a motherly tone. "Make yourselves useful over here, would ya!"

"Yes, ma'am, right away ma'am!" Pete fired back, as if responding to a drill sergeant. "I'll get it, guys. Don't get up, just sit and relax," he added sarcastically toward Jake and Cole who had yet to move a muscle. "I'll get this thing a-blazin'," he said and began to light the newspaper underneath the teepee of wooden pallets they had constructed. They had brought enough wood to last them until early morning. And knowing them, they'd probably need it.

"The beach, the beach, the beach is on fire!" sang Pete, jumping around like an Indian dancing for rain.

"We don't need no water, let the motherfucker burn!" the other five of them joined in on the old club song of the early nineties.

"Oh, great gods of beach bonfires everywhere," Pete started in, "may you bless this pile of wood, this fine food and this cold beer." Everyone knew he was clowning around, but he kept a straight face in the middle of the spoof. He and Cole had the two best poker faces you've ever seen. "We ask for your skies to stay clear and your breath to stay warm. And we ask your assistance, oh, great bonfire gods, in getting these women really drunk and horny!" he ended, finally cracking a smile.

Just as Pete finished talking, the fire cracked loudly and he jumped back about two feet. The rest of the gang got as big a kick out of that as they did anything else. He sat down, grabbed a beer and he took a joint from his unbuttoned top shirt pocket. "Anyone in the mood to partake of an herbal offering to bonfire gods?" he asked, holding the joint up like it was some sort of talisman.

"You know, Pete, as funny as this may sound, I'm not," Cole said with a curious tone. "Did I just say that?" he asked himself, but said it out loud, and he looked over at Jake.

"Nothing wrong with that, Cole," Hope said, feeling good about Cole's choice.

"Anyone else?" Pete asked, but he didn't get any takers. "Well, then I shall join you in your nonstonedness, but I can't tease the bonfire gods, so this is for them," he said, throwing the joint into the middle of the flames.

The guys had smoked pot on and off for the last few years although none of them did it all that often. They weren't like many of their other friends in school who had to get high before doing nearly everything. And contrary to the speeches made during Drug Awareness Week, they never moved on to other drugs. Their attitude toward getting high was strictly social. They didn't drink or smoke to hide from any personal problem; they were just having fun and could take it just as easy as they could leave it.

"So, Debra, since you are the newcomer and we haven't picked on you yet," Cole began, "we'll have to start with you. First question for everyone: What's the strangest place you have ever had sex?"

"Well, it didn't take long for the conversation to get to sex. Hell, the sun's only been down for ten minutes," Jake said.

"The strangest place, huh? Well, let's see. Probably on an airplane," Debra revealed.

"No way! You're in the mile high club?" Pete shouted. "I am jealous."

"Airplane! Talk about the friendly skies, huh?" Cole commented. "What about you, Jake?"

"I haven't really been the sexually adventurous type. Geez, I don't know," Jake said. "Probably the couch. Hell, I've only ever had sex with Jennifer." Jennifer was Jake's girlfriend during high school and they dated for about a year. She was a good girl, but didn't always treat Jake well. He deserved better and he knew it. So, after graduation, they went their separate ways. "Hey, but the lights were on!" he added, laughing. Jake was comfortable with the fact he wasn't that experienced. He was only nineteen, and to him there was no rush. He had loved Jennifer and she was his first long-term girlfriend. Sex was special to him and he wasn't a big-time player like Pete or Cole. It was important to him to only be with people he really cared about. Most people in a group of nineteen-year-old guys would have made fun of someone with old-fashioned views like that, but not Pete or Cole. They had a tremendous respect for each other in a really unique way. They understood Jake and he understood them.

"What about you, Susan?" Jake asked.

"I'll tell you when it happens. I haven't ever had sex. Well, not intercourse anyway," she clarified.

"Get the fuck outta here," Pete said in a quick, high-pitched voice.

"No really, the last American virgin in the flesh," she added.

Jake didn't say anything then but that really impressed him about Susan. He hadn't known that before—they had never discussed it—but it was nice. He wouldn't have thought anything less of her either way, but there was something special about wanting to wait for the right person. Just as Jake was getting the warm fuzzies in the pit of his stomach, thinking about how pure a girl he was dating, Susan said, "But I once gave a guy a blow job on a Greyhound!"

"Well, the ladies certainly do have all modes of transportation covered. If Hope has a story about a car or a horse, we'll be complete!" Pete exclaimed.

Hope looked at Cole and they both laughed.

"What are you two laughing at?" Jake asked.

"Well, we actually did do it in a car," Cole added.

"That's not that unusual," Debra remarked.

"Yeah, what's so strange about that? Even my parents have probably done it in the back seat during the good old days. You know, up on Inspiration Point, or no doubt something like it," Pete said.

"Well, we weren't in the back seat," Cole continued, "and we weren't parked. We did it going through the drive-thru at McDonald's."

"Some young kid was riding by on his bike and saw us, and he started cheering," Hope added.

"Well, that's a new one," Pete said. "I can just picture Hope ordering. Can I have a Quarter Pounder—oh, my God—with cheese and a large—oh, Cole, don't stop—order of fries and a hot—oh, baby, yeah, I am hot for you—apple pie?"

Laughing hysterically, Cole said, "And Pete, what about you, ya big stud? Are there any excursions you haven't already told us about? If not, I know a few that are worth mentioning."

"The most unusual place I had sex was probably at that festival our senior year. Remember that girl Cindy, who I dated for a while?" he asked. "Well anyway, she and I did it in the fun house. You know, the kind with all the mirrors that make funny shapes?"

"Now, that's what I call a fun house," Hope added.

"Yeah, it was pretty wild. Well, we were busy getting hot and sweaty, and I was starting to feel all proud of myself because I was looking at us in the mirror while we were movin' and grovin.' It was one of those funky mirrors that make everything look bigger and longer," Pete said. "Yeah, you get the idea. Why I turned my head and looked around I'll never know. Unfortunately, the other side had a mirror that made everything look smaller and all weird. It made Cindy's head look like an alien. You know, small on the bottom and all big on top. It freaked the hell out of me, it really did. I couldn't go out with her anymore after that. Hell, I could barely talk to her."

"That's hilarious. I don't think you ever told us about that," Jake said, starting to laugh. "No wonder you can't watch *The X-Files*."

"Hey, a little close encounter never hurt anyone," Cole joked. "At least your alien experience was better than all the reports you hear about. You know, 'Billy Bob gets abducted in the field behind his trailer park and the aliens perform an anal probe.'" Everyone laughed and Cole switched subjects. "Toss me a beer, would ya, Pete? Oh yeah, I meant to ask you, when is your next home game?"

"Next Friday, my bruddha. Are you guys gonna come?" Pete asked.

"We wouldn't miss it for anything," said Hope. "The Pete Landry Fan Club may be small but it has enthusiastic members!"

"Is membership still open?" asked Debra, smiling at Pete.

"I am sure we can squeeze you in," Hope replied.

They sat back relaxing and talking, enjoying the famous San Diego cool night air. The moon started to roll gently toward the top of the sky. It was a beautiful moon, only few days past full. It lit up the sky, giving a halo of light to each passing cloud. The whitecaps of the ocean picked up the glare, as if someone were painting a silver crest on top of each wave.

"I just love the nighttime weather here this time of year," said Debra. "It's just too bad the water isn't warmer; it would be great to take a little dip."

"We've all had a handful of beers. That ought to add at least a couple of degrees to what the water temp actually is. I'm up for it," Cole said, getting up and making his way toward the water. Reluctantly, the others followed, probably more to talk him out of it than to actually join him.

"You're crazy," Pete said, stepping into the water. "It can't be more than seventy degrees, if that."

"So what? It's only a little chilly. We're all here, and it will be the perfect ending to a great night," Cole argued.

"Oh, just do it, you big wuss," called Susan, who ironically was the first to shed her clothes. The moon glowed on her pale white cheeks as she ran for the water.

"Whoooooooaaaaaaaa! Look at her! I like this girl, Jake," Cole said. He was hopping on one foot as he tried to get out of his shorts to follow her.

De-clothed, each of them made their way into the chilly waters. "Damn, this is cold," said Jake, holding onto Susan to stay warm. They jumped around dunking each other and Cole did a handstand on the sandy ocean floor.

"Hey, a…Cole," Pete began, "you may want to keep yourself below water, buddy. You know that things tend to shrink a bit when they get cold, right? But do what you want. That's just a suggestion; take it or leave it, Mr. Stubby."

"I've got to agree, honey," said Hope, "there are definitely more attractive things than an upside-down naked man."

They played around in the water in the moonlight until their bodies were numb. It didn't matter. Even with the cold they had a great time. The whole thing was so spontaneous and they felt so alive. Alive with friendship. Alive with emotion. Alive with life itself.

CHAPTER FOURTEEN

Cole knocked on the office door and got a welcome from the professor. "Well, I decided to splurge today," said Cole. "I thought you might like some of the good stuff instead." He handed the professor a large coffee from Starbucks.

"And a wonderful gift it is, Mr. Anderson, thank you," replied Professor McIntry. "So how is your spirit today, my friend? Tell me about what's been happening since last time we talked."

"I am doing pretty well, professor. I have been feeling much more comfortable. I mean, I am still searching for answers on a lot of questions, but it just seems different. Like it's all right to be searching and that things will work out," responded Cole.

"Wonderful, Cole, just wonderful," commented the professor.

Cole started in again. "As you know, two of my good friends are also in your class, my girlfriend Hope and one of my best friends Jake. And the girl Jake is dating took your class two years ago. Her name is Susan Powers—"

Cole paused because he saw the professor's eyes widen at the mention of Susan's name.

"Susan Powers…what a fine soul she is. Now there is a young woman who understands spirit. She will do great things in the world, Cole. Believe me when I tell you that. Tell her I said 'hello.' She comes and visits now and then, but I haven't seen her in a few months."

"Sure thing, and you're right. She is a great girl; we like her a lot," added Cole. "So it's been interesting because the four of us can talk about things. And although we are all coming from different perspectives, we can understand each other. Then I have my friend Pete—and whatever girl he's with at the time—and it's like he's our anchor, you know, keeping us attached to the ground so we don't float off into space."

"An anchor is good. You are fortunate to have that in a close friend," the professor said.

"Yeah, Pete is great. Just when we think he's isn't paying attention, he surprises us. Sometimes it gets to the others that he doesn't take things too seriously, but to me, I think that's the lesson. Hell, I know I take things too seriously sometimes. God, I love him. I don't know what I'd do without him." Cole slipped into deep thought and then continued, "Since I made some decisions about how I wanted to be in my relationship with Hope, I am feeling so much better. There was always this confused, almost chaotic feeling inside, but it's gone. It's gone in relation to Hope and me anyway. It makes so much sense to me now. It's as if I caused all the confusion by not being committed to a particular direction. I mean, there are a lot of reasons why I love Hope, but I guess I figured if I really wanted to be in the relationship, I needed to do my part. Just like sports or anything else: doing it halfway sucks," Cole concluded.

"Well, Cole, you have grown wiser right in front of my eyes. You have just figured out one of the main reasons so many people feel life is such a struggle," the professor said feeling proud of his young student. "Most people don't know what they are committed to or where they are headed. This is why I feel it is so important, as you grow and develop, to search your soul for what really makes your heart sing with joy, to find a purpose in life you feel is worth working toward. When you truly have that understanding in your heart, life becomes much simpler to live. Without purpose, it's like you are out in a boat in the middle of the ocean without a destination. What direction do you go in? How fast should you go? Should you stop to have a fruity tropical cocktail in the Virgin Islands?" Cole laughed as Professor McIntry smiled.

"Just like that boat, Cole, when you choose a path to follow in life, you then have a framework or focus point to make decisions against. When you are faced with a choice, you can always ask yourself: Does this get me closer toward or further away from my purpose? Those without a purpose turn left, then right, then put up the sails when there is no wind, then try to go against the strong current—and they wonder why they are in the same place ten years later. There's no mystery to it: When you have formed a strong self-identity, something will either support who you are or not, and choices become increasing simple if you stay true to yourself. Do you understand what I am saying, Cole?"

"Yeah, it makes a lot of sense," Cole replied. "But honestly, professor, I have no idea what I want to do with my life. So when you talk about a life purpose, I understand what you mean and all, but it's just not part of my reality right now."

"It can be as big a part of your reality as you want it to be, Cole," the professor answered. "Look, it's not exactly necessary that you choose today what you will do your entire life. Hell, *I* don't even know what I will be doing for my entire life, but I do know how I want to go about it, and the kind of person I will be in the process. What you do and how well you do it will be a reflection of who you are. If you work to gain a clear understanding of yourself and the type of qualities you choose to have as a human being and you take action, you will either find or create a profession that completely supports what you stand for. That I can promise you with all certainty," concluded Professor McIntry. "So tell me about your progress with the meditations, Cole."

"Well, as you said, focusing is getting a bit easier," responded Cole. "As you know, when I first started, everything seemed to get in my way. I was trying to think of nothing and all I could think about was everything. Either something on my body would itch, or I didn't feel comfortable how I was sitting, or I'd have thoughts zooming through my head about all kinds of crazy stuff. But over the last couple weeks, I have been able to clear out a lot of that and I can stay relatively blank for a few minutes. Like you suggested, I have been focusing on a small pinpoint of light. I've tried different colors, but light blue seems to work the best for me. Do you think the meditation has something to do with my feeling better about things?" he asked.

"It would probably be ignorant to think they weren't related," said the professor. "As I told you, at the beginning when you are first working to gain more control over your thoughts, the benefits are subtle. I think you are making great progress and you seem to be thinking more clearly. I think you are ready for the next step," he paused and looked directly into Cole's eyes. "I want to teach you how to create some of the circumstances you desire in your life. You are closer to it than you think. Do you remember the class, it was either last week or the week before, when we talked about cause and effect?"

"Of course," Cole replied.

"I want to take that a step further with you today," the professor continued. "In class, we talked about the necessity of keeping your thoughts focused on your desired outcome, instead of focusing in on what you don't want, right?" Cole shook his head in agreement. "What do you think would happen if you actually started to preplan the events?" Cole looked up puzzled. "Cole, what if you could help write the script before it actually happened?" the professor asked.

"I don't know if I am following you," Cole responded. "Are you saying we have the ability to actually create something? I mean, from out of nowhere?"

"Not from nowhere—from out of your mind, son. Which is exactly what most people will think you are for believing it, out of your mind," the professor added. "So we are going to add some specific statements and mental pictures to the meditations you have been doing. So far, you have been practicing on how to clear off your internal screen, and you have come a long way, considering how much crap is on most people's screens. Now, we are going add fuel to this creative process. I want you to continue with your five minutes a day, just in the silence, doing your best to release everything and not think about anything. That will continue to allow you to sharpen your focus and increase your energy.

"But what I also want you to begin to do is create some basic events or circumstances you want to happen and write them down. Write them down as a positive affirmation, making sure to claim ownership not only in how you write the statement, but also in your intent as you say them. I want you to read them out loud at least three times a day. And during your meditations, I want you to start visualizing these events occurring. In your visualizations, I want you to use as much detail as possible. Actually feel what it would be like had these events already happened. Take in the entire experience in your imagination. Be grateful and believe with all of your heart that the events have already happened. Are you following me so far?" asked the professor.

"So, it's kind of like daydreaming, but with a purpose?" Cole asked.

"It's exactly like daydreaming with a purpose," the professor replied. "Then, just as you put effort into this creative process, you need to completely detach yourself from the outcome. Affirm, visualize and believe, and then leave the process to happen. Any thoughts or feelings about whether or not it will actually happen come from a place of lack or disbelief, and will only hold you from the events you are co-creating."

"I think it's kind of funny that my old teachers used to yell at me for daydreaming, telling me if I didn't pay attention I wouldn't learn anything," began Cole. "Now you're telling me it is something I should be doing. I guess it makes sense though, and fits in with what you are saying, because I could always create a better place in my imagination than where I actually was at the time."

"Cole, as you learn more about yourself and how the creative laws of the universe work, you will find we did many of them very naturally as young children. I believe the knowledge of these creative laws is inherent in everyone when they are born. Then we either keep this intuitive knowledge close to our heart and develop it, or we are educated away from believing in its validity. If you think about when you were a child, you understood the incredible power of your imagination," the professor continued. "Hell, as kids, most of us lived in our imaginary world and to us it was real, as real as anything else was. The fact that most people think they learn how the 'real' world works as they grow up is a dangerous disease we need to stop.

"Hold onto that creative ability and those childlike views of people and the world as you grow in years and gain life experiences. Do this and you will not only have an internal relationship that makes your life a joy, but you will also attract external circumstances to match your dreams. Don't ever grow up, my friend. At least, do not grow out of your belief that we live in an unlimited and abundant world."

"No problem, professor," replied Cole. "That one I can handle. So, what you want me to do is write down a few things I would actually like to happen, read them at least three times a day, and during my meditations, actually visualize these events happening? Is that pretty close to what you mean?"

"Precisely, Cole."

"That sounds pretty simple and it actually sounds like fun," added Cole.

"It's both fun and simple, but it takes some discipline. Not any more discipline than it takes to watch TV, but nevertheless, it does require a commitment on your part," Professor McIntry concluded. "I do want to caution you though. This creative process, when fueled with action in the direction of what you desire to create, always works. So there are two things you must understand. The first is that you must be careful to visualize only what you truly desire. When you attach your emotions to something and really feel the experience, your creative power is incredibly strong. Make sure you clear your screen first, okay?"

Cole nodded.

"And second, Cole, although this process never fails—just as gravity never fails to hold us to the earth—you must be patient with the results. Time has no relevance in your internal world. Simply accept your affirmations as already accomplished facts, put action out in the direction of your goals, and let the universe take care of the rest," the professor said.

"There has got to be more to it than that," said Cole. "If it were that easy, why doesn't everyone have exactly what they want?"

"Who said it was easy?" asked the professor. "It's a simple process, yes; but it definitely is not always easy. Why more people don't have the kind of life they want is a good question. In my opinion, most people are so buckled by fear and limiting beliefs about themselves and life that it makes it almost impossible to succeed. They tend not to work to improve their own abilities and as a result, the external world keeps slapping them in the face. And other times it is simply that they either don't know how, or don't believe they can do it.

"Keep in mind, these processes and disciplines aren't taught through school and rarely do people learn them from their parents. So when most people are presented with this information, it is a bit hard to swallow. Some disregard it completely as not being real and others try it but don't really believe in it, which as you know will never work. Still others believe in it for a while, but because their results don't happen as quickly as they like, they think it doesn't work."

The professor looked Cole squarely in the eye and said, "There is no short cut to personal success. It takes energy, focus, a strong commitment and the ability to follow some basic disciplines. Being an average, unhappy, unproductive slob requires far less effort. But the rewards of being an empowered human being who is completely alive are definitely worth the effort."

"Yeah, I hear ya, professor," began Cole. "For me anyway, I think that once you get a taste of success, it's hard to go back. Since I have been working with you and taking the class, everything just seems different. I seem to be happier, more relaxed and much more focused. I also feel I am making better choices, in my relationship with Hope, for example. Like my friends and I were talking about on the beach the other night, I guess I'm looking at things through different eyes."

"Indeed, you are, Cole. Indeed, you are."

CHAPTER FIFTEEN

The week flew by as if the days had only eight hours each. Cole awoke to the sound of music coming from the living room and the clickety-clank of pots and pans in the kitchen. It was Friday morning and he could smell that someone was actually making breakfast, a rare occurrence at their house. Cole sat up in bed and pulled his list of affirmations from the drawer in the night stand. He got himself comfortable and relaxed, then began to read them out loud as he had each morning, noon and night for the previous week. Since this was all new to him, he decided to start small, with just a single affirmation. After thinking about what was important to him—and what he really wanted—Cole finally created a statement that got him excited and that he could visualize in detail and with emotion.

"Hope and I are having a fantastic time as we enjoy a weekend getaway," he said to himself in a soft voice, being sure to really back his statement with full belief. He repeated it again, then closed his eyes, took a few deep breaths and drifted into a relaxed state of meditation. He visualized himself lying on the floor of a cabin with Hope, somewhere in the mountains. In his mind's eye he saw an incredible, dense forest from the deck surrounding the front side of the cabin. They lay embracing, with U2 playing softly in the background. Putting himself fully into the experience, he felt the gentleness of her touch and the warmth they had created together inside the cabin. It was perfect, truly—

"Honey, do you want some breakfast?" Hope came through the bedroom door, followed by the smell of eggs and coffee. "What are you doing?" she asked, seeing him sitting in bed, propped up against the headboard.

"Just thinking, Hopes," Cole responded. He jumped out of bed before any more questions came up. "Yeah, I'd love some breakfast."

They sat in the kitchen as the glowing San Diego sun warmed the room around them. Cole ate quietly. He wasn't really paying attention to what he was doing or the fact that Hope was sitting right next to him. His mind drifted to Professor McIntry. He thought about how incredible it was to have such a fantastic professor, and that he was actually getting to spend private time with him. He thought about how much had changed in his thinking over the last four or five months, and how differently he was beginning to view things. He thought about how many people were in the professor's class and, as the professor had predicted, how most of them didn't pay much attention to what he said. He thought about the new affirmation and visualization technique he had started and how excited he was about the whole concept. He wanted to believe it worked. How incredible it would be to choose and shape the circumstances of his life. As he sat thinking, getting excited, he began to hear something faintly, inside his mind. Then it became louder. He could hear it clearly now—

"Cole! Cole!" Hope was calling out. "Earth to Cole! Come in, Mr. Anderson."

"Huh, uh, what?" Cole stammered.

"Are you all right?" she asked.

"Yeah, I've just been thinking a lot lately. It's all good, hon, really," Cole replied, regaining a grip on his senses as his attention came back to the moment. "Okay, so what's the plan for tonight?"

"Well, Susan is picking up me and Debra and we'll meet you and Jake here at six o'clock. Pete said the game starts at seven. So, we'll get over there a bit early and get some good seats."

"You know, Hopes, I am a pretty lucky guy," Cole began. "There's not a lot of guys out there who can say their girlfriend gets just as excited about a baseball game as they do, if not more so."

"You are lucky, buster, and you remember that," Hope ordered playfully. "I've been around sports all my life, you know that. As far as this game goes, it's mainly because of Pete. I can take it or leave it when it's just baseball, but this is Pete-ball!"

"Yeah, they win tonight, and they're in the playoffs," Cole added. "All right, so six o'clock it is. I'll be here! I'm off to class. See ya, baby," he said, pulling Hope close and giving her a nice, big kiss goodbye. It was the kind of kiss that makes you wish you were saying hello instead and that you had the time to finish what you started.

"Are you sure you've got to go to class?" Hope could feel his kiss all the way to her knees. "We could just stay here all day and I could, ah, educate you."

"Oh you are a bad girl, Hopes, a very bad girl, and it's part of why I love ya. But I've gotta go to class. I'll see you tonight," said Cole, letting the door close behind him.

"All right, I think we need to send some energy to Pete; he's a bit off tonight," said Cole as the Titans came off the field to start the bottom of the seventh inning.

"Yeah, I can't believe he booted that grounder. That's not like him at all," added Jake.

"He'll come back. He's up this inning, isn't he?" Hope asked.

"Yeah, as long as they get someone on, he's up fourth this inning," Jake replied.

The game was a seesaw battle; both teams led at different times. The Titans jumped out to a two-run lead in the third inning, only to see the L.A.–based visiting team come back with three runs in the fourth. A two-run homer by the Titan catcher in the sixth put the Titans back in front. But unfortunately Pete's error in the seventh inning put a runner in scoring position and a sacrifice fly scored a run to tie the game.

In the bottom of the seventh, the Titans lead-off batter hit a lazy fly ball to short right field and it dropped in for a single. The next batter drilled a line drive into left that dropped right in front of the charging outfielder. Unfortunately the base runners were held at first and second. The energy in the stadium built as the home team had a chance to retake the lead. "Strike three!" shouted the home plate umpire as the next batter went down on three straight pitches. Pete made his way from the on-deck circle into the batter's box. He was 0 for 2 and had yet to make good contact.

"Let's go, Pete, whooooooooooooooooooaaaaaaaaaaaa!" shouted Debra. She stood up, threw her arms in the air and shook from side to side. The rest of the gang enjoyed her enthusiasm.

"Come on, Pete!" Jake and Cole blurted out together. "You da man!"

The runners took their leads and the pitcher fired a fastball chest high, right where Pete liked it. He took a big swing and hit a sharp ground ball that headed just to the left of the shortstop.

"Get through! Come on! Get through, ball," Cole tried to coach the ball into the outfield.

The shortstop scooped it up and flipped it to second. And the second baseman fired it to first for a double play to end the inning.

"Aw, shit!" said a disappointed Jake. "Man, we could have used that one to get through."

"Hey, I'm gonna grab some water. Anyone want anything?" Susan asked, getting up from her seat.

"Why don't you just bring a couple up? I'm sure someone will drink them," Cole suggested.

"I'll go with you then," Jake added, following Susan off the bleachers and down toward the concession stands.

The Titans were down by two runs going into the all-important bottom of the ninth. After getting two runners on base and advancing them to second and third with a sacrifice bunt, the Titans had the tying runs in scoring position with only one out. The next batter up hit a long fly ball that was caught on the warning track. The runners tagged up, scoring one run and putting a runner on third with two outs. Pete walked slowly up to the plate.

The coach and the rest of the team were all standing at the edge of the dugout, clapping their hands and shouting encouragement to the young star who had performed so well for them all season. But now, Pete found himself in the biggest game he had ever played: the life or death of the team's season rested squarely on his shoulders. If he managed to get a hit, he would tie the game and give them a chance to win—at the very least, the game would go to extra innings. Otherwise, the long and hard-fought season would be over.

Pete got comfortable in the batter's box, and the home plate umpire pointed to the pitcher, giving him the cue to resume play. The pitcher, working from the windup, fired a breaking ball that caught the outside corner for strike one. The tension mounted in the stadium. Everyone was on their feet: both teams, both coaches and all the spectators, especially the small but loud Pete Landry Fan Club.

"Let's go Peeeeeeeeeeeeeete!" the five of them shouted at the top of their lungs.

The pitcher stared down Pete and tossed the second pitch. Pete turned on it and ripped a line drive right over the third baseman's head. It was curving but looked like it would stay fair. The crowd screamed as Pete took off for first. The ball kept hooking more and more and landed, just fowl, midway up the left field line. A big "ahhhhh" was heard throughout the stadium as Pete returned to home plate, now behind in the count, no balls and two strikes.

The pitcher wasted a couple low and outside and had run the count even, at two balls and two strikes. The energy in the stadium was electrifying. He wound up and fired a fastball. Pete stepped into it with a good hard cut and the ball popped into the catcher's glove for the third strike. The game and the season were over. Dejected, Pete walked back to a disappointed dugout and was greeted with hollow condolences and empty sympathy for his effort.

"Poor Pete," Hope said, for she felt her friend's pain.

"Yeah, it really sucks," Cole added. "The guy hits three twenty-five for the season, but he's gonna be remembered most for that strikeout. It's just not right."

"Well, we'll cheer him up tonight," suggested Susan.

"That's exactly what we'll do," concluded Jake. "Think the team will still get together tonight?"

"They probably will, but I wouldn't expect it to be the most festive of parties," said Cole.

"We'll either make it festive or make our own," added Hope.

Later that night, the three couples sat around on the deck outside the team's "victory party." It was to have been a celebration, so they had purchased plenty of refreshments and picked a house that was farther away from campus. Although the team wasn't exactly blaming Pete for the loss, he was being hard on himself and was throwing back quite a few beers in the process.

"Man, I just can't believe I frickin' choked like that," Pete said, slurring his speech.

"Hey, Pete, come on. Take it easy on yourself. You are a big reason the team was even in that game tonight. You kicked ass all season," Cole said, trying to lighten his good friend's spirit.

"All for naught, *amigo*. All for naught," Pete replied. "You know it, bro. You're as good as your last day. Just like Mike Tyson. He whupped people's asses for years, and how does everyone remember him? As the sick bastard who bit off Evander Holyfield's ear."

"That's different, Pete," Jake argued.

"Is it, Jake? Is it really that different?" Pete answered. "Look, guys, I appreciate what you are trying to do, really, but I'm gonna need some time on this one. I have never failed at anything I cared about, and yeah, I know I didn't fail the season. But I definitely failed tonight, so let me vent a bit more and I'll eventually work through it."

"Just as long as you know we are here for you, Pete," Hope said. "You know you can count on us for anything." The rest of the group nodded in agreement.

"Thanks, guys; it means a lot. I appreciate it," Pete responded.

They sat there and made small talk for a while. No one brought up the game anymore, because they all knew Pete was right. No one, with the exception of maybe Cole, really knew what he was feeling. But they could understand why he didn't want anyone trying to cheer him up. It wasn't a cheer-up kind of situation. He had to work through it on his own, and in his own time.

"Hey, Hopes and I are going to take a walk. Anyone want to come along?" said Cole. He stood up and Hope pressed her hand firmly into his. No one else accepted the invite, so Cole and Hope made their way off the back deck into the field behind the house. They walked hand in hand, enjoying the night air, looking up at the endless specks of light covering the night sky.

"They never cease to ease the pain," said Cole, referring to the spectacular stars above them. "I think Pete could use the magic hammock right about now, huh?"

"He sure could. It's tough, but he'll work through it," Hope added.

"Yeah, he'll be all right."

As they walked along, Cole had an incredible feeling of *déjà vu*. Hope, the rolling grass, the beautiful stars, the warm night air—it all seemed so familiar to him. It was like he had walked this exact path before, but he didn't know when. He could just feel the familiarity of the experience. As he searched his thoughts and emotions, a beautiful butterfly flew gently in front of Hope. It danced around from side to side, performing a circus in the wind for them. It was gorgeous and surreal; the colors were vibrant and bold. The butterfly spun around and landed softly on Hope's shoulder. And in that instant, Cole knew exactly where the feelings of familiarity came from.

"My God, Hopes!" Cole exclaimed, not sure if he even believed what he was about to say.

"It's just on my shoulder, Cole. It's okay," she replied, confused.

"No, you don't understand. Hopes, do you remember that dream I had a little while ago, when I woke up screaming in the middle of the night?" he asked.

"Ah, I think so."

"Well, this is it, it's happening right now," Cole replied.

"What do you mean, 'this is it'? What's happening right now?" Hope responded, even more confused.

"I mean I dreamt we were walking in a green field just like this one, and we were talking and there were tons of stars out and the moon was a tiny sliver, just like tonight," Cole said frantically as he pointed at the small crescent moon above. "At first it just felt weird and I couldn't place it. But then that butterfly fluttered by and when it landed on your shoulder I knew it," he paused. "Baby, this is exactly what happened in the dream. The colors were the same and it landed directly on your shoulder."

"That's incredible," Hope said, intrigued by this whole new turn of events. "So, what happened next?"

"That's where it gets kinda bizarre. The butterfly turned into a huge, black buzzard—you know, a vulture. It was awful. And that's when I woke up," he added. "Oh yeah, and right before that, there was a huge crash over the hill. I remember because it was so piercingly loud, I felt it through to my bones."

"Well, I don't know about a loud noise," Hope started, "but I am pretty sure this butterfly isn't going to turn into a buzza—"

Hope's voice was drowned out by a huge crashing sound, which came from over the hill in front of them. They couldn't believe what they heard. Frozen in disbelief, they stared at each other not knowing what to do. Could they have fallen asleep somehow while looking at the stars and this was just another dream? As they stared at each other, not understanding what was happening, voices coming from the house jolted them back to reality. Then turned and ran toward the hill in the direction of the crash. As they got to the top of the hill they saw a car, half-mangled, with the front end bent like a horseshoe around a telephone pole.

"Oh, my God, Cole! That looks like Debra's car!" Hope screamed.

"Go to the house and call nine-one-one!" Cole shouted as Hope tried to gather her wits about her. "Go, Hope! Do it now! Go call nine-one-one and tell them to get an ambulance over here!" Cole screamed. There was no time to calm her down first. As Hope turned to run back to the house, Cole ran down toward the car. Sure enough, it was Debra's car, and it was nearly totaled. Both front tires were sticking straight out and the hood was a crumbled ball of twisted metal on the ground about five feet away. As he got closer, he could see someone moving on the passenger's side. He looked in the window and saw Debra, groggy and wincing in pain, but apparently with only minor injuries. He tried to open the door, but it was smashed shut.

"Just stay put. The ambulance is on its way. The door won't open and I'm afraid if I move you, I may hurt you worse," Cole said and as he did, he looked up and saw Pete, unconscious in the driver's seat.

"Ah Christ, Pete," Cole said, running around to the other side of the car. His best friend's body was twisted around the steering wheel, his head and one arm hanging out the shattered window. He had evidently flown forward into the windshield; he was bleeding profusely from a head wound and his leg was wedged up under the dashboard. "Oh God, Pete! Oh, my God, Pete!" Cole cried, reaching down to put his fingers on Pete's neck and praying desperately for a pulse. Although faint, it was still beating.

With blood covering his hand, Cole screamed, "You stay with me, you son of a bitch! Don't you fucking die on me! Oh, Pete, come on, come on."

Within minutes that seemed like days, the ambulance sirens got louder and the tires screeched to a stop. The paramedics made their way over to the wreckage. "Please get back, son!" one of the medics shouted to Cole.

Cole stood there frightened and helpless, watching his two friends being worked on. He couldn't believe it. What had just happened? Jake, Hope and Susan came running up from the house, just in time to see Pete and Debra being put in ambulances. The four of them stood there, speechless and numb.

CHAPTER SIXTEEN

For the first few miles of their drive to the hospital, the four of them sat in the jeep, staring, thinking, but not saying a word. Cole was driving, but he just peered ahead as if in a trance. Hope slid over to comfort him in the best embrace she could afford at this point; to give any more of herself would completely drain her.

"Jake, did you call Pete's parents?" Cole asked.

"Ah, yeah, I did. They are on their way down here," Jake replied.

"That's good. Okay, they'll be down here in a few hours. That's good. Okay," Cole spoke, but was obviously disconnected from his words. He was frantic and in shock. "We can call our parents from the hospital, but they don't need to come down. No, they can stay home. Yes, we can call them from the hospital. Dammit, I can't believe this happened!" he screamed, pounding the steering wheel with his hands. "What happened, guys? Who the hell let him drive?"

"No one let him drive, Cole, and don't start implying anything. We all know this sucks. It sucks real bad, but no one here caused it!" Jake shouted.

"Yeah, I know. I'm sorry. It's just crazy. It's so damn crazy. So what happened?" Cole asked again.

"I don't really know," Jake began. "When you two went for a walk, we were just sitting around for a while talking. Then Pete said he wanted to be alone and he walked out front. About ten minutes later Debra went after him to see if he was okay. The next time we saw him was when…ah…um…it was when they were being loaded into the ambulance." He paused, took a deep breath and looked up toward Cole. "Ah shit, Cole, he didn't look too good, did he?"

Cole, fighting back the tears, said, "Naw, not really. He was unconscious and his head was bleeding a lot. It looked like he hit the windshield, and it looked like he hit the steering wheel hard too. My God, all I can see in my head is Pete lying there all bloody. I can't get it out of my mind. He's got to be okay, he's just got to be okay!"

No one spoke again until they arrived at the hospital. They were in shock and no one knew what to say. One of their best friends was under the hot bright lights of an emergency room operating table, possibly still unconscious. It didn't seem right. It didn't seem real or fair, or anything else for that matter.

At the hospital, their request to see their friends was denied. The four of them sat impatiently in the cold, bland public waiting room. It was half past one in the morning. Silently, they watched the sick and injured crowd the emergency room.

In one corner stood a man holding his elderly wife tightly. She was shaking and looked like she could break in half at any moment. A young Mexican couple sat across the room with their young son. He had his hand wrapped in a homemade bandage and had obviously cut it pretty badly. People were moaning in pain or coughing, just altogether miserable with their current situations.

"I've got to get out of this room, guys. Let's find the cafeteria, okay? It's bound to be less depressing than this," Cole suggested.

No one objected. They all felt the same way Cole did: The room didn't make waiting any easier. They found out the cafeteria was down the hall, so they told the receptionist to please direct the doctor and Pete's parents there. Cole made it very clear they wanted to see Pete and Debra as soon as the doctor said it was allowed.

"Does anyone want a coffee?" Hope said, making her way over to the machine. Knowing they would probably be there for a while, three semi-conscious nods came from group.

"Man, I can't stand this waiting. They've got to be able to tell us something!" Jake exclaimed. Susan put her arm around Jake to try to provide some comfort. Hope started crying and buried her face in Cole's shoulder.

"I don't frickin' get it. Just when I think I'm starting to understand something about how this crazy world works, Pete gets frickin' mangled in a car. Why? Why did this have to happen?" shouted Cole.

"You'll drive yourself crazy trying to figure out 'why,' Cole," Susan commented. "I know you guys all know Pete better than I do, but the three of you have become better friends to me in the last few months than anyone else in my entire life. I know this is absolutely horrible, but trying to figure out why something like this happens will just tear you apart inside."

"Yeah, but you didn't dream this was going to happen," Cole snapped back.

"What? You dreamt Pete was going to get into an accident?" Jake asked, puzzled.

"Well, not exactly," Cole began. "I didn't know it was Pete. A couple weeks ago, I had a bad dream that woke me up in the middle of the night and tonight, what I dreamt about actually happened. When Hopes and I were walking out in the field behind the house, I had this incredible feeling of *déjà vu*. I mean, it was weird, guys. Every detail was the same. The colors, the smells, everything. In the dream, a beautiful butterfly landed on Hopes shoulder, just like tonight," Cole continued. Even though she had already heard this, Hope looked at him just as intently as did Jake and Susan. None of them, including Cole, knew what to make of it. "So this butterfly lands on her shoulder and then we hear this thunderous crash from over the hill, just like tonight. As we turned to run to see what it was, the butterfly changed into a huge, black buzzard. It spread out its wings, and squawked. It scared the shit out of us. That's when I woke up. Except for the buzzard thing, everything else I dreamt actually happened tonight, in the same, exact detail."

"That's insane," Jake said. "That's the most incredible thing I've ever heard of. How the hell do you dream the future?"

"I don't know, man, but it's freaking me out," Cole replied. "Susan, you're the smart one in all of this stuff. What the hell does it mean?"

"I don't have a clue, Cole," she replied. "It could be a bunch of different things, but I don't really know."

Just then the door came flying open and a nurse walked in the cafeteria. Still startled by Cole's story, they all jumped.

"The receptionist told me you were the ones who were here with the two car accident victims. Is that correct?" the nurse asked.

"Yes, yes, that's us," Cole responded quickly. "The two people are Pete Landry and Debra Ross. How are they? Can we see them?"

"Not just yet," the nurse replied. "The girl, Debra, is okay. She has some abrasions and some bruised ribs, but she'll be just fine. She's really fortunate she was wearing her seat belt."

"What about Pete, miss? What about the driver, Pete Landry?" Cole asked nervously.

"Are any of you family?" the nurse asked.

They all knew that wasn't what they wanted to hear. Hope, Jake, and Susan just stared, not knowing what to do.

"I've known him since he was five, dammit! Pete is family!" Cole shouted angrily.

"Cole," Hope jumped in. "Miss, we're all like family here. Pete's parents are on their way down. We'd really appreciate anything you can share with us," she added, knowing it wasn't the nurse's fault.

"He has a laceration on the front of his head that we will be able to mend fairly easily. But he has some internal bleeding coming from a lacerated liver, and we are about to take him into surgery to see if we can stop the bleeding. That's all I can tell you right now. I'm sorry. Another attendant should bring Debra down shortly," the nurse ended.

They said "thank you" and just sat there staring at the door swing back and forth. Their eyes focused on the door. It was as if this old, creaky door was fanning their fears, and heightening their tension and pain. The room grew cold and an empty feeling filled the entire cafeteria. They were too stunned to cry and too sad to move. They must have sat in dead silence for almost an hour. No one even looked at each other. Each of them, although physically present, had drifted away into their own thoughts. The silence was broken as the doors swung back open.

"Cole, Hope, Jake, what happened? Have you heard anything about Peter?" Mrs. Landry shouted hysterically.

"Have you heard anything, anything at all?" Mr. Landry followed.

"Yeah, um, the nurse told us he has a lacerated liver, and they took him into surgery about an hour ago," Cole answered slowly, still in a daze.

"Oh, my God! My Peter! How did this happen? How did this happen?" Mrs. Landry continued.

Hope rushed toward her and threw her arms around her neck. They embraced, both women trying to hold back tears, trying to stay strong.

"We don't really know what happened exactly, Mr. Landry," Jake said. "We were at a party after the game. Pete didn't play real well and he was kinda depressed. He had been drinking some and he had gone for a walk to be by himself. His date, Debra, went to go find him and the next time we saw them they were being taken here by the ambulance."

"There was a girl with him? Is she okay?" Mr. Landry asked.

"The nurse said she'll be all right. She just has some bruises and stuff," Cole replied.

"Oh, excuse me. Mr. Landry, Mrs. Landry, this is my girlfriend, Susan," said Jake.

"Hi, folks. My prayers are with Pete," said Susan, offering her hand.

"Hello, Susan. Thank you. Sorry, we didn't mean to be rude," Mr. Landry said speaking for the two of them.

"No apology necessary," Susan responded. "I understand."

Just then the door was slowly pushed open again and everyone turned to see who was entering this grief-stricken hospital cafeteria. A nurse was walking with Debra, helping her along. Debra had a bruise on her forehead that was starting to turn color, a butterfly bandage next to her right eye, and some sort of bandage on her ribs.

"Hey, everyone," she said, walking in.

"Are you all right, Deb? How do you feel?" Hope asked, giving Debra her sympathy. They made a path for Debra, eased her over into a chair, and gathered around her.

"Yeah, I'm okay. I'm just really sore," she replied. "What about Pete? How is he?"

"He's in surgery. We're all just waiting now. These are his parents, Debra," Cole said.

"Are you sure you're all right, honey?" Mrs. Landry asked.

"Yes, thank you."

"So, what happened, Deb? Are you up to talking about it?" Cole asked.

"Yeah, that's fine. Um well, I walked out after Pete to see if he was okay, and ah, I found him on the lawn by the driveway. He was just lying there, staring off into nowhere," Debra said. "We started talking and he said he wanted to go to this spot. It's one of his favorite places in the city; he's taken me there a few times. There's this hill over by the campus that we go to. He likes to look at the stars. He says it lets him clear his mind."

Hope, Jake, and Cole looked at each other in disbelief. Their best friend, seemingly so removed from that part of their life, had been right there with them all along—only he had been there on his own. While they were engaged in conversations about the purpose of life and what the universe had in store, Pete'd had his own discoveries all along, his own version of Cole's magic hammock. Together they took a deep breath and wondered what else they might not have known about Pete, or about each other. What other areas of their life did they have in common, but for some reason, some fear, or some inhibition, didn't share with each other?

"We were coming around the corner and a dog ran out into the road," she continued. "Pete swerved to miss it and he lost control and we headed right for a telephone poll. The next thing I remember was Cole trying to open the door."

"A fucking dog?" Cole shouted. "A goddamned dog? You've got to be kidding me. My best friend is upstairs getting surgery because of a damn dog?" Cole was a steaming cauldron of emotions and this new bit of information just cranked up the heat.

Although they all knew it wasn't just the dog that caused the accident, and that the alcohol obviously had a big effect, no one said a thing. None of that really mattered, with Pete still upstairs. Whether it was a dog, too many beers, the depression from the game, or something ridiculous like the smell of Debra's perfume that caused Pete to lose control of the car was irrelevant. Nothing—not a speech on drinking and driving or a pep talk from the baseball coach—was going to save his life right now. It was up to the doctor and God. Two big hands helping two small hands perform the surgery. Twelve years of undergraduate school, medical school, and residency prepared someone to be a doctor, but did it prepare a person for this incredible amount of responsibility? They were all so involved they didn't see or hear the doctor walk in behind them.

"Mr. and Mrs. Landry?" the doctor asked. "My name is Dr. Stevenson."

"How is Peter? Can we see him?" Mrs. Landry asked quickly.

"Can I speak to you folks alone, in the hall here, please?" the doctor requested.

"Sure, Doctor," said Mr. Landry, and they followed him into the hall.

Left to wait in the cafeteria, the gang was anxious for some sort of information, some word as to when they could go see their friend.

"No! No! No!" cried Mrs. Landry from the hallway. They looked at each other; somehow they all knew what that cry meant. Mr. Landry pushed open the door and slowly walked toward them, dragging his feet. Mrs. Landry remained in the hallway crying.

"Peter's liver was lacerated badly and, ah, they couldn't, um," he stumbled over his words, "stop the bleeding. He died a few minutes ago."

"Oh, my God. No, this can't be happening!" Cole shouted. Hope threw her arms around him and cried uncontrollably. He broke away from her, flung open the swinging door, and raced past Mrs. Landry and the doctor. Cole ran through the hallway and out of the hospital screaming, "Why? Why him, God? Why the hell did you take him?"

CHAPTER SEVENTEEN

Knock, knock, knock echoed through the silence of Professor McIntry's house. Knock, knock, knock. Cole pounded on the front door as if he thought the professor could get there from his bedroom in five seconds, after being awakened at four-thirty in the morning. Knock, knock, knock. Cole rapped again.

"I'm coming. Who's there?" asked the professor.

"It's Cole Anderson, professor. I know it's late, but I really need to talk to you," Cole pleaded.

The professor unlocked the door and opened it just enough to see Cole's face, distraught, confused, angry, and dejected. He knew at once this was more than a late night drunken revelation. It was plain to see the tortures of Cole's soul had risen to the surface. "Come in, Cole. Here, have a seat. I'd ask how your spirit is, but it is clear it has taken a bit of a beating. Can I get you something to drink?" the professor asked.

"No, thank you. Well, maybe some water would be good," replied Cole. The normal request at a time like this would have been for the strongest alcoholic beverage he could find, but Cole knew that wouldn't help. No buzz would bring Pete back. No intoxication would make him forget the picture he had in his mind: Pete half hanging out the driver's side window of Debra's car, with blood all over his face.

"Professor, my friend Pete, you know, the one I told you about who plays baseball," just then Cole stopped talking. It hit him that he could no longer talk about Pete that way. It didn't seem right he would have to talk about his nineteen-year-old friend in the past tense. Fifteen years of doing things together, experiencing them in the present tense, and now that time was gone. Gone forever, never to return.

"Yes, I remember you talking about him," the professor answered, snapping Cole out of his daze.

"He just died," Cole said, not believing those words had come from his mouth. "He was in a car accident last night and died while in surgery, professor." Cole paused, expecting the professor to respond, but he just sat there looking into Cole's eyes. "We were at this party after the game," Cole continued. "Pete had a pretty bad game yesterday and he was kinda down on himself. But we were all just hanging out at this party. We were drinking a little and things seemed okay. I mean, he seemed okay. Hope and I went for a walk and that was the last time I...I talked to him.

"His girlfriend Debra said they went to go drive to a place she said Pete liked to go when he wanted to just think and clear his mind. It was this hill somewhere by the campus and he used to just lie there and look at the stars. That's, ah, pretty crazy, 'cause um, ah, that's part of our lives we never shared with each other. You know I have this hammock at my parent's house. When things got kinda chaotic and tough to deal with, I would just lie there and look at the stars and think. Hope and Jake and I call it the magic hammock."

The professor cracked a little smile.

"I just can't believe he's gone. It's not fair, professor. He was my best friend. We didn't get to talk about the stars and how they made us feel and what they meant to us. We didn't know that about each other. Dammit, I can't believe this has happened."

"I am going to put on some coffee. Would you like some?" the professor said, getting up and walking toward the kitchen almost as if nothing had happened.

"Ah, sure, I guess," Cole replied.

"My father died last year, Cole. It can be a tough spot to work through," Professor McIntry continued, talking loudly over the running water. "Dealing with death is a process like everything else. But you never told me much about Pete. What was he like?"

"Professor, I don't know if I can. I mean, he just died about an hour ago. It's difficult to even talk about it," Cole said reluctantly.

Blatantly ignoring Cole's hesitation, the professor repeated, "What was he like?"

Cole sat there on Professor McIntry's couch, looking up toward the ceiling as tears filled his eyes. He tried to bring his thoughts away from the bloody mess of the night before, to the friendship and experiences the two of them had spent fifteen years building. What was going to happen now that Pete would no longer be around? How would it affect everybody? He drifted off into his own world and, for a moment, forgot where he was and that the professor had asked him a question.

"Oh, um, Pete was the best," Cole said finally. "We met when we were four or five and have been inseparable ever since. Well, um, ah, until now anyway." He took a deep breath, "I mean, we've had a few little arguments over the years…but for the most part, we never even really had a big fight. I guess, kind of like me, Pete was sort of a character. You could never really tell what he was going to do, except that you could usually guarantee it would be fun. He was the kind of guy you wanted to be around all the time, because he'd always lift your spirits. If you were down for some reason, he'd pick you back up. If you were excited about something, he would get more excited about it than you were once you told him. He always supported me, always. Ha, humpf," Cole said, cracking as much of a smile as he could muster. "Pete was the best wingman of all time. There was no one better to have with you if you were out 'lookin for love,' if you know what I mean."

The professor smiled and shook his head.

"He had this whole theory about being shallow. Well, that's what he called it anyway. It was actually just that he tended not to think too deeply, at least most of the time. He figured if he didn't want much, didn't question much, or didn't need much, he was pretty likely to be happy. But at the same time, he wasn't lazy. He worked hard at things that held interest for him, and he usually did really well. And you know, Pete was pretty damn happy most of the time."

"Sounds like a smart guy to me," the professor said.

"Yeah, that's true. I guess he was sort of wise in his own way," continued Cole. "I wish I had gotten to talk to him about all this. It's like there was a whole aspect to Pete that I didn't really know, an aspect I'll never know."

"It's true, Cole, that you won't be able to physically be with Pete anymore," the professor began, "but the things you're saying are about getting to understand the spirit of Pete, and his spirit hasn't gone anywhere. It's here for you whenever you want it to be."

"I don't know if I understand what you mean," Cole replied.

"Close your eyes, Cole, and relax," Professor McIntry requested.

"I don't know, professor. I don't think I'm in the mood for meditation right now," Cole answered sharply.

"Have I ever worked with you before in a way that you didn't benefit from?" the professor asked just as sharply.

"No, never," Cole responded.

"So, close your eyes and relax. Get comfortable and take a nice, slow, deep breath. Allow yourself to become totally relaxed. I may ask you some questions, so just nod to answer." The professor paused and let Cole take a few more deep breaths, bringing himself into a completely relaxed state of awareness. "Now, I want you to think of one of the happiest times you can remember that you and Pete shared. I want you to remember this experience in the fullest detail."

Cole's mind shuffled through the endless files in the database of fun experiences they had had, growing up together all through middle school and high school. There were so many happy times. Then his mind settled on an experience that stood out above the rest. "I remember our senior prom," said Cole. "Jake was with his girlfriend, Jennifer. Pete had brought a girl he had been seeing named Heidi and of course, I was with Hope."

"Remember all the people who were there," urged the professor. "Where you were, how you felt, and what the weather was like. Remember any smells or fragrances and the specific emotions you had. I want you to feel what it was like to be there. I want you to take yourself back there right now. Feel all the emotions, feel all the joy and happiness and the bond you have in friendship. Experience everything as if you are there right now," the professor continued. "Now, Cole, remember every detail, especially how you felt and how your senses were enlivened. Take yourself there. Experience it completely."

The professor sat and watched Cole as he brought himself back to the experience. Cole watched the events of that memorable night zip through his mind in fast forward. It was a perfect night, no problems, no trouble, just a great time with great friends. It wasn't the fun they had in the limo that he was fixed on; it wasn't the dance when he and Hope were named king and queen, and it wasn't even the party they went to afterward. It was what happened late that night after the party that he remembered the most, and that made him the happiest.

One of the seniors who lived down by the beach had hosted the after-prom party, which was filled with a couple dozens intoxicated classmates. It was the last get-together for many of them and people were going crazy, partying, dancing and singing. Someone played the piano. As the night went on and 6:00 A.M. approached, the party started slowly dying down. They had set up two big limo buses to take them to breakfast and then to Disneyland the next day. This had been kind of a senior class tradition at their high school for as long as anyone could remember. Just as everyone was piling onto the bus, Pete grabbed Cole and Jake and suggested they do their own thing instead of going off with the rest of the group. The three couples did a U-turn and headed off for their own post-prom adventure. They quickly decided to go down to the beach and watch the sunrise. They stopped off at a local convenient store and picked up the essential breakfast supplies. They bought orange juice, six coffees, and a few assorted packs of tiny donuts.

Kicking off their dress shoes, they walked onto the beach and out toward the water. Dressed in full tuxes and long gowns, they looked like they were filming a music video. Hope was in a sexy, yet elegant, emerald green dress that hugged her womanly curves in all the right places. Heidi wore a traditional black dress Pete loved as it subtly showed off her cleavage. And Jennifer looked stunning in a cream colored, high-necked, open backed dress with her auburn hair pinned up, which made her look very regal indeed. The guys strutted through the sand in traditional black tuxedos, with cummerbunds and bow ties that matched their dates' dress selection. If someone were watching from afar, the sight would have been surreal.

The guys laid down their rented tux jackets on the sand to create a makeshift blanket to sit on. Then they all lay back and took in the ending of their high school years with the dawning of a new day. The sunrise on the California beach was magical. There is something mystical about the sun rising from behind, as it gently spreads its blanket of hazy morning light across the patiently waiting beach below.

The traditional Southern California light cloud cover started to burn off as the sun rose into the sky. Mother Nature slowly gave birth to another brilliant day with a light film of dew to cover the world and a soft, cool breeze along the shoreline of her powerful waters.

Sunrise creates an entirely different feeling from sunset. Fresh experiences come to clear away the past. It is nature's way of bringing a new day forward and shouting "You have an open canvas…paint on it what you will! Use any colors and means you want. Paint nothing or create a masterpiece, because this is your canvas, this is your life, this is *your* new day, and you can do with it whatever you choose."

They sat on the beach and talked, just talked. They talked about all their crazy high school times, about how the guys had stayed friends since they were little kids and how rare that was. They spoke about going off to college together, although none of them knew what they actually wanted to do when they graduated, or even what they wanted to major in. They talked about how things were about to become much different for them, how even though the guys and Hope would still be together, everything would be different from how it was in high school. Although they had taken advantage of it all along the way, they knew high school was easy compared to what they had in store for them.

They talked about graduation from college and the "real" world. And what the hell were they going to do then? They talked about different jobs they might want to do, but none of the jobs seemed like they would be exciting enough to do every day for the rest of their lives. They all agreed the best jobs would be ones that allowed them to keep their friendships and have more good times on the beach in the future. There was so much to talk about. There was so much to do. There was so much excitement matched with fear about what was to come.

Cole remembered the salty air that was filled with a light fog. He remembered the smiles that were painted across everyone's face throughout the entire morning. He remembered feeling so close to everyone. And he remembered that he could just look over at Pete and lock eyes with him for just a moment, and they both understood. They understood how valuable their friendship was.

"Just keep yourself in the emotion of the experience," the professor began again. "Just let yourself go and feel it."

And he did. It was as if that night was happening right now. He was in the experience. He could feel and sense his friends around him. He felt the cool morning breeze blowing through the light fog. He was there.

"Now, I want you to look at Pete and simply stay with the feelings and emotions you are experiencing with him as you live in this memory," the professor said. "It feels good, doesn't it?" Cole nodded gently. "You can sense each other's energy, can't you?" He nodded again. "Now, keep this feeling with you, and when you're ready come back to this room."

Cole gently brought his mind and spirit back to the professor's house to join his physical body and slowly opened his eyes. His body tingled all over, but he felt good.

"He was with you, wasn't he, Cole?" Professor McIntry asked.

"It was incredible. I mean, it was like I completely relived the experience," Cole replied. "I really felt it."

"You can feel Pete with you any time, and you don't have to relive a past experience. You can simply enjoy his presence. He may not be here physically, but he will always be with you, as long as you want him to be, and probably even sometimes when you don't," the professor stated, smiling. "My father is with me all the time."

"Thank you, professor. This will help. I still can't believe he's gone," Cole said and his eyes filled with tears. He paused, then shouted, "Ah shit, professor! I didn't tell you the most screwed up part. I dreamt the whole damn thing."

"What do you mean exactly?" inquired the professor.

"I mean I dreamt the whole night, to the last detail. Okay, this is what happened. A few weeks ago I had this dream that Hope and I were walking in a grassy field under the stars, and then this butterfly started flying around us and landed on Hope's shoulder. Just as we heard a huge crash over the hill, the butterfly turned into a massive, black buzzard. When that happened, I woke up in a sweat," Cole explained. "Professor, that is exactly what happened last night, minus the buzzard of course, and the crash we heard over the hill was Pete's accident."

The professor looked at Cole, carefully listening to what he said.

"What's all this about, professor? It's really freaking me out," begged Cole.

"Well, I am certainly not the expert on dream interpretation, but I've done some studies and some research, and I can share what I know," Professor McIntry began. "Dreaming about the future isn't that abnormal, so it shouldn't 'freak you out.' In fact, you've probably done it before, but you just haven't realized it. Do you remember studying about Julius Caesar? Well, if you remember the story, his wife Calpurnia dreamt about his assassination, not once, but twice in the same night. Even Abraham Lincoln dreamt of his own death just two weeks before he was killed in the balcony of Ford's Theatre. You have heard of ESP, right, Cole?"

Cole nodded in understanding. "Sure, extra sensory perception."

"Dreaming about the future often works very much the same way. Sometimes, something will lodge in your subconscious and then be released while you're dreaming; and sometimes you'll pick up on the thoughts of someone else, like telepathy. Other times—which sounds more like what has happened with you—the dream is actually a vision of future events triggered by your connection with the universal consciousness while dreaming."

"Come again, professor?" Cole requested.

"It's often been called 'hypersensory' perception, as opposed to extrasensory perception and it's a very real phenomenon. I once attended a lecture by a man named Robert Moss, who has dedicated most of his life to the study of dreams. It was a fascinating program and I learned a lot about the 'realness' of dreams, their meaning and symbolism."

"Are you saying that if I would have paid closer attention, I could have stopped this from happening?" Cole asked in a strong voice.

"Anything's a possibility, Cole. But in this case, I don't think there was anything you could have done. This was your first experience with this and you didn't actually see who was affected in your dream. Don't even put a thought to the accident being your fault because you had a dream about it. Blaming yourself doesn't solve a thing," the professor continued.

"Look, Cole, I don't think this is the time to go into a lesson on dream interpretation. At this point, just acknowledge what happened and don't disregard it as a coincidence. If you want any helpful advice, I would simply tell you to do your best to work through this experience. Although it may be more difficult right now than it would be to suppress how you feel about it, you'll gain so much more by actually dealing with it. I'll be thinking and praying for you, your friends, and Pete's family. But for now, you've been up all night. Why don't you go get some sleep, okay?"

"Yeah, all right. The others should probably be back from the hospital by now," Cole stated. "Professor, thanks. You're a good friend."

"So are you, Cole, and I don't want you to worry about coming to class this week. Take your time and I'll see you when you're ready," responded the professor.

"I appreciate that, but I think I'll come just the same if it's okay with you," Cole replied. "The lessons I've learned through you have helped me so much, and I think it will be good for me right now."

"Good enough. Well then, let me know if you need anything, Cole. And remember what we did here tonight. Your friend is as close as you want him to be."

CHAPTER EIGHTEEN

"Cole, where have you been? Are you okay?" Pete's mother cried out. She jumped up from the kitchen chair when Cole walked in the front door. It was late morning and no one had gone to sleep yet. Mr. and Mrs. Landry had been sitting around the kitchen table drinking coffee and talking with Hope, Susan, and Jake, and Debra was resting her aching body, fast asleep in one of the back bedrooms. None of them wanted to be alone, and you couldn't blame them.

"Yeah, all right. I went to see Professor McIntry," Cole replied. His answer was no surprise to his three friends, but the Landrys were a bit confused. "He's one of our professors who has helped us through a lot of personal stuff this year. I guess he's sort of like a father figure, guru, friend, and spiritual counselor all wrapped up in one. Anyway, he sends his love."

Everyone was still pretty numb and they were moving slowly, not really paying much attention to things around them. They were only about half there, with the other half of their psyche focused on Pete and how this shock had seemingly come out of nowhere. Each of them ran nostalgic movies over and over in their minds. Emotions bounced from joy to sadness as they remembered good times with Pete, and that there would be no more of them. They missed him already, and a day hadn't even passed since he had died.

"Well, if you kids are going to be okay for now, we'd better start heading back up north, honey," Mr. Landry said. "There's not much more we can do down here. We have a lot of things we need to attend to at home. Let's stop by the hospital on the way and finish whatever we need to there, and then head straight back home."

"All right, I just want to check on Debra before we leave," Mrs. Landry replied. "She's so far from home and she's had to go through this without her parents being here. Just give me a minute." She headed toward the back bedroom where Debra was resting.

"We'll let you all know when the funeral arrangements are—in a few days," Mr. Landry said. Cole could tell Pete's father was trying hard to hold back his emotions in front of everyone else. Cole knew what was going on because that was the way he had been raised by his father, to be strong and not show emotion.

Somewhere along the way, probably when he started getting serious with Hope, Cole started changing. Bottling everything up was tearing at him from the inside out, ripping slowly at his soul. And only he had the key to his self-induced torture chamber. Like Cole's father, Mr. Landry lived by a fairly old school philosophy. Men were men: tough and unemotional. Cole looked up into Mr. Landry's eyes, which were clearly holding back tears. He stepped toward him and gave him a big hug. The two men embraced. This was something Mr. Landry wasn't used to and it was almost too much for him.

Fighting the tears back, he said, "Ah, guys, we'll speak to you, ah, shortly. Tell Mrs. Landry I am waiting for her out in the car." It was clear he didn't want everyone to see him cry. He turned and walked out to the car with streaks of liquid sadness running down his cheeks. A moment later Mrs. Landry came out, said her goodbyes and they were gone.

The next day passed as if time were standing still. It seemed like an eternity from dawn to dusk, with each single moment having a separate space. It was like sitting in a study hall during the last period of the last day of school before summer vacation. The clock seemed to go backward, and it was as if your whole life could have been lived in the time it took for those last twenty-five minutes to click by.

The two couples and Debra talked little about what had happened. It was understood: Talk when you want to and get support if you need it. Privately, each of them reflected on their moments with Pete, how he had influenced their lives, and what they would keep with them forever.

Cole shared with them his meditation experiences with Professor McIntry and encouraged them to find their own special moment, so they could all keep Pete close by. They talked about whether or not they wanted to go to Professor McIntry's class and they all decided they did. So, the following morning, Hope, Jake, and Cole found themselves sitting in the lecture hall waiting for the professor to arrive.

Suddenly the lights in the auditorium went out. There were no windows except for the tiny one in the door, which was blocked off, and it was dark, really dark. A light from up in the corner of the room shone down onto the crowd of students. It was almost blinding to look at, and it seemed to come out of nowhere.

"You've just died," said the professor, who must have concealed his presence in the room earlier. "This is the tunnel of light that many people who have had near death experiences talk about. Do you go toward the light? If you do, where will you be?" The lecture hall was completely silent except for the sound of the professor's voice. It was obvious the students were tense and possibly a bit nervous. The professor continued in a deep, full voice, "When you go through the light are you to be judged for your actions and either elevated to heaven or banished to hell? Are you afraid of the light? Are you afraid of death?" Suddenly the light went out and the room was again dark. Some startled students gasped. After a short pause, they heard, "Are you afraid of life?"

It was silent for a moment. Then a projector started and the word "life" appeared in big, bold, green letters on a white background, on the screen at the front of the room. It stayed on the screen for a while in the silence. Then the word "death" took its place, in big, red letters against a black background.

Then they started switching back and forth: life, death, life, death, life, death…and it stopped on life. A picture of a newborn baby appeared, then a beautiful green meadow, then people smiling and laughing, then a rosebud opening, then a bicyclist raising his hands in victory, then a football team holding a trophy high in the air, then a mountaintop, then a wave cresting in the ocean…then it froze on an eagle flying.

Abruptly, death flashed back up and was immediately followed by a tombstone, then a car accident, a bloody battlefield, Jesus on the cross, a plane crash, a village ravaged by famine, a scorched forest, a polluted river, and a news scene of a murder.

Then the scenes started flashing quickly back and forth, one representing life then one representing death. They flashed back and forth, faster and faster, dozens and dozens of pictures, some incredibly beautiful, and others completely horrifying. Then, as suddenly as they started, they stopped, and the room was again dark and silent. For nearly a minute the room was still and filled with emotion. Then, in a flash, the bright light at the corner of the room turned back on.

"The human ego is obsessed with death," the professor's voice boomed out of the background. "It fears it and does everything it can to avoid death of any kind. Since so many of us live under the influence of ego, our society is afraid of death, petrified of it to such a degree that we are aware of it in almost everything we do." The lights in the auditorium came back on and the big spotlight was turned off. "Who here is afraid of dying?" he asked.

To no one's surprise, much of the class raised their hands.

"We've all had someone close to us die. Whether it was a grandparent, parent, brother or sister," the professor looked right at Jake, Hope, and Cole and added, "or a good friend. And you know what? It's going to happen again. I guarantee it. Everyone here will lose someone they are really close to at some point in the future. The only way you can avoid it is if you die first, and that certainly isn't a good alternative." The professor looked into the crowd of students and saw they were clearly disturbed by the discussion so far. "Who feels uncomfortable with this conversation?"

Again most of the hands went up.

"I promise you this," he continued, "if you try to relax and keep an open mind, you will not only feel much better about death, but also incredibly better about life."

The professor paused, smiling, then said, "Let's start by figuring out why we are so afraid of death in the first place. So let's have it. What are some of the causes of our fears or any other major emotions about death?"

"It's unknown," a student called out.

"Okay. Good start," said the professor.

"Because death is final," shouted another voice. "Life usually gives you another chance, but death is permanent."

"Good. What else?"

"Religion makes you fear death," called out another student. "Well, a lot of them do anyway. Many of them are so strict that you live in fear of Judgment Day."

"Excellent. Certainly, many of the Western religions do just that. Mr. Anderson, what would you say is a possible cause of fear of death?" the professor asked.

Cole had been staring straight ahead, listening to everything being said, but also thinking about everything that had happened. "Maybe, professor, it's because it's such a big change. It's a shock to the system. One day someone's here, the next they aren't. I think it's easy to fear major changes."

"Absolutely, and in the physical world, death is the final change. In the physical world, everything eventually dies, although many things begin a new life as part of a cycle. The seasons change as winter dies and spring is born. The caterpillar seemingly dies only to be born again as a beautiful butterfly. Old stars die and new stars are born—" the professor was interrupted.

"But that's not true!" exclaimed a student from the back. "Old stars never die, professor. They just fade away."

The student laughed and everyone in the room joined in, including the professor.

"Indeed, the 'last hurrah' as they say, the 'final chapter,' the 'last dance,' the 'end of the road.' Our Western cultures have been obsessed with death since life began," the professor stated. "Well, what if you didn't fear death? What if you looked at death as simply a part of the evolution of your spirit?" The professor looked up to see if his rhetorical questions were sinking in. "We've talked a lot about spirit all semester, right?" The class nodded in understanding and agreement. "We've talked a lot about spirit because we have said that each of us, in our purest form, is essentially spirit. No matter what religion or faith you follow, and whether you call it your soul or your spirit, it is agreed that when we strip away the physical body, and the emotional shell that has developed over the years, we are left with this essence. Could we agree that this essence, which I will call spirit, never dies? In other words, physical death does not mean spiritual death?"

Again the class nodded, following along closely with the professor's thinking.

"Okay, so now we've agreed on what actually transpires at death, which is that the spirit lives on. I don't want to get into where the spirit actually goes, because that is completely a matter of opinion, generally based on what religion you believe in. Whether you believe that your spirit will ascend to heaven, or descend to hell, or live in the water or the trees, or stay in the cemetery, or haunt those who were mean to you during your life, or reincarnate as your dog Rover is completely up to you. What I want to do is help you get to a place where you are comfortable with whatever it is that may take place. Why? Because it is only when you can move away from your survival-based fear of death, that you can really and truly experience the wonderful joys of life and be at peace with who you are."

"It's probably why many people who have near death experiences or are faced with a life threatening disease take on a whole new appreciation for life," commented a student.

"I think there's more to it than that," suggested Cole. "Maybe the person who has had the near death experience has actually seen and felt what the afterlife is all about and can understand the whole process, and that would definitely give someone a new appreciation of life. But I know that many times the person who has a life-threatening disease appreciates life more only because they are still afraid to die, and now they actually know their time is limited."

"I think you both have valid points. Well, let's talk a little about how others view death. The Greek philosopher Epicurus said: 'Death, the most dreaded of evils, is therefore of no concern to us; for while we exist death is not present, and when death is present we no longer exist.' Then there was Italy's Giovanni Falcone who stood up to the Mafia. He said—very appropriately for today—'He who doesn't fear death dies only once.' And, of course, good old Woody Allen has a line: 'Death should not be seen as an end but as a very effective way to cut down expenses.'" With that, the professor got a laugh out of the class.

"William Penn said: 'Death is but crossing the world, as friends do the seas; they live in one another still.' And one of my favorite authors, J. D. Salinger, wrote in *The Catcher in the Rye*, 'Boy, when you are dead, they really fix you up. I hope to hell when I do die somebody has sense enough to just dump me in the river or something. Anything except sticking me in a goddam cemetery. People coming and putting a bunch of flowers on your stomach on Sunday and all that crap. Who wants flowers when you are dead? Nobody.'" Again the class chuckled with amusement.

"Let us finish with William Shakespeare from *Julius Caesar*, 'Cowards die many times before their deaths; The valiant never taste of death but once. Of all the wonders that I yet have heard, It seems to me most strange that men should fear; Seeing that death, a necessary end, Will come when it will come.'

"So from humor to eloquent prose, different people of different cultures have different views on what death is all about. A common thread, though, is that we shouldn't fear it," added the professor. "Some cultures mourn death, others celebrate it; some honor it, while still others deny it.

"I want to encourage all of you to explore and identify your own feelings about death," the professor continued. "Don't run from it and don't use euphemisms to describe it—that does nothing but perpetuate the fear. Like many other things we've discussed this semester, do not buy into someone else's story. Figure out for yourself what you really believe."

"Professor?" A strong yet disturbed voice came from the class. It was Hope. "I understand what we have been talking about, and I do believe that our spirits live on. I haven't come to terms with reincarnation yet; I am still figuring out what the whole afterlife process means for me. I also understand that fear has been built up around death in our society, as something that takes away from ego.

"But here's my question..." Hope collected herself, as she had just gotten to the difficult part. "What about when you know you are really going to miss someone? You know, when they have been such a huge part of your life, you just can't imagine them not being there anymore. When you have someone you are really close to, there is a special place in your heart for them. When they die, it's like a part of your heart dies with them."

The room was silent and still, filled with people who were not really present. They were all in their own individual worlds. At that exact moment, everyone was taken back to a time when someone close to them had died. They felt it all over again. Professor McIntry's attention was riveted on Hope; he empathized with her and Jake and Cole. He felt the emotions of every student in his class all at the same time. He took on their emotions. He took on their pain.

Professor McIntry looked deep into Hope's eyes and said, "Don't let that part die, my dear. Allow it to grow, and keep him with you forever. I am not going to say you won't experience some sadness and pain—I think all of us are experiencing some emotion about it right now—but you can have him with you any time you want.

"There's nothing easy emotionally about the death of a good friend or a parent, or anyone or anything else for that matter," the professor continued. "We immediately feel we have this void in ourselves. We all can remember good times when we were really young that stand out more than others do. If we focus on one of those events, we can see and feel and experience the spirit of that event all over again. The spirit of the one who has died is very much the same; it is always with you when you want it to be. That doesn't mean you won't miss them, but it does mean they will always be a part of your life, if you choose to keep them dear to your heart."

He paused, then asked, "Do you understand, Hope?" She nodded. "Do the rest of you understand as well?" They nodded too.

Professor McIntry sat on top of his desk, looking out at the emotion-filled faces of his students. After a pause he asked, "So would you forget me if I died?"

"Not possible!" shouted a student.

"Oh, everything's possible, right?" suggested the professor. "Well, I'll tell you what. If any of you are still around when the rumors of my death aren't greatly exaggerated but actually are true, I want a huge party. It's already part of my will. It is my request that all of my friends and family hold a huge celebration, marking my spiritual graduation. I don't want tears when people are remembering me; I want laughter. I don't want misery; I want joy. I want the grandest celebration, because I have had the grandest of journeys."

"You sound like it's gonna be next week, professor," stated Cole.

"You never know, my friend; it very well may be," the professor replied. "I personally don't think it's my time yet, but if it is, get ready to party." He looked at his watch and added, "Although my time isn't over yet, our class time is. *Adios, amigos.*"

CHAPTER NINETEEN

The phone rang and woke up Cole and Hope. "Ah, umph, hello?" Cole sputtered, clearing the dust from his throat and the dreams from his head.

"Cole, this is Mrs. Landry. Did I wake you?"

"Ah, oh, no, it's okay," Cole responded. He reflected on how people always ask if they woke you up when they know they did, and how we always deny it. "So how are you doing, Mrs. Landry?"

"I am managing, Cole, thanks. How are all of you doing?" she replied.

"All right, I guess. We're all kinda still in a daze," Cole answered "So, when is everything happening? I am sure there will be a lot of people coming up from campus."

"That's wonderful," Mrs. Landry commented. She was comforted by the fact that so many of her son's friends were planning to come to pay their respects. "The funeral is going to be tomorrow at one o'clock. Peter was never big on churches, so we've arranged to have the entire service out at the cemetery. I think he'd like it better that way."

"You're probably right," said Cole, "I'll let the others know the details, and we'll see you then."

"That's fine. There's one more thing, Cole. Mr. Landry and I would like you to present the eulogy for Peter. You were his best friend and we'd be honored if you would consider doing that for us—and for Peter."

Cole sat up sharply in bed and fell silent.

"Are you there, Cole?" she asked.

"Ah, yeah, yes, I'm here," he replied. "It's just that, ah, well, it's a bit unexpected. I'm a little overwhelmed."

Mrs. Landry didn't respond.

"But um, actually Mrs. Landry, it would be my honor. Thank you for asking me," Cole said, taking a big, dry swallow as he fought back his nerves. "See you tomorrow."

Cole's nervous anticipation went beyond performance jitters. He was honored to do it, but this was different from ordinary public speaking. This time he wasn't going to be giving a speech on the Vietnam War or debating the pros and cons of abortion and the death penalty. No, this time he was going to be sharing with loving friends what the life of his best friend had meant to him. He had to open his heart in front of people, not just his mind. He was going to be vulnerable, completely out there. No one knew Pete better than he did and he owed it to him not to hold back.

"The Landrys want me to give Pete's eulogy," he said to Hope as he hung up the phone.

She waited for him to finish.

"The funeral is tomorrow," he continued. "We've got to tell the others, and the coach, and I'd like to tell Professor McIntry as well. That class he gave the other day really helped."

"I know it did me," Hope said. "Like he said, looking at the whole process of death differently won't eliminate the feelings that come up, but it sure helps you process your emotions a lot better." She paused. "So, how do you feel about giving the eulogy?"

"Okay, I guess. I mean, like I told Mrs. Landry, I feel honored to be asked," Cole began. "It's just…well, it's just that I want to make sure I do it well. Pete deserves it. He deserves the best. I just hope I can give it to him."

"Oh, honey, I understand what you mean. But I've got to tell you, it amazes me that everyone around you sees you so much more clearly than you see yourself," said Hope. "You are good at everything you do, Cole. You should know that by now. Part of your beauty as a person is that you are unsure at times. That innocence is so special. Baby, you are going to do a great job. I know it. The Landrys know it. And Pete knows it. You know if you just speak from your heart it will all be fine."

"Yeah, I know. Thanks. Everyone needs some reassurance from time to time."

"I know that better than anyone," Hope replied quickly, thinking of her own recent transitions. "If you need any help with the eulogy, you know you can always come to me."

"Yeah, I know, Hopes. Thanks. But I think this is one I need to do on my own."

"I understand," said Hope warmly. "Hey, Jake and Susan stayed over at her house last night. Do you want to call them and meet for breakfast?"

"Sounds good. Why don't we see if Debra is up to it as well?" Cole added.

"Perfect. I'm going to jump in the shower—you're welcome to join me if you want," Hope said invitingly.

She got out of bed, shed her underwear, and strode naked across to the bathroom.

"Ahhhh, ummm, I don't know," Cole said as he faked a big yawn. Hope looked back at his pitiful display of noninterest, shrugged her shoulders and threw her panties at him. "Just kidding, honey. Watch out! Slippery when wet...here I come!" He jumped up, kicked off his boxers and made a mad dash after her.

An hour later, the five of them sat at their favorite breakfast spot drinking coffee and looking over the menu. The restaurant was a dive, featuring a dozen or so tables and eight bar stools around a half-circle counter. It was an old-fashioned diner that hadn't been kept up.

Although the place was open twenty-four hours a day, they had never eaten anything but breakfast there. Everything on the menu—only about seven different items—was under four bucks. And since they had spent many early mornings there after late nights out, they had all tried everything.

"How are you feeling, Debra?" Susan asked as she stirred milk into her coffee.

"Physically, not bad. But emotionally, I'm kind of a wreck," she replied. "I know I didn't know Pete nearly as long as any of you did, but I really liked him, and I know he liked me more than he let on. He was full of life and it didn't take long to feel comfortable around him. Thank God I was knocked out during the accident, 'cause I don't think I could have handled looking at him like that. It still hasn't sunk in; everything is so surreal."

There was a general silence, then Jake spoke. "I know what you mean about everything being surreal. It's weird. I mean, I know Pete's gone, but I can still feel him. It's like what we talked about in class the other day: He hasn't gone anywhere."

"Yeah, I know. I keep thinking he's supposed to come in any minute and pull up a chair next to Debra," expressed Cole.

"I think it's really good that we can talk about Pete in this way," Hope started. "We might not think we are dealing with things very well, but I suspect we are. I think it's important to keep his spirit alive within our circle of friends. He'd want it that way. You know Pete…he never missed a social gathering."

"Hell, he started most of them," Cole added.

Jake started laughing lightly to himself, then a little louder.

"What's so funny, mister?" Susan asked, poking him in the ribs, his ticklish spot.

"I was just thinking about when Pete and I first met Debra. Pete pulled that corny James Bond act on her and she made him melt in his seat. It was one of the few times I have ever seen Pete struck speechless by a woman!" Jake concluded.

"Now, that is surreal!" Hope said, laughing, and everyone joined in.

They ate breakfast and sat there sharing stories for hours. It was good to be together again and release some of the tension. Cole told them about the funeral plans and they agreed to take two cars and caravan up there. As Hope had pointed out, they were dealing with Pete's death pretty well. But every so often, they would look toward the empty chair where Pete would have been, or they would think what Pete would have said about this or that, or how he joked. And in that moment, they missed him. They missed him dearly.

CHAPTER TWENTY

It was an incredibly beautiful afternoon. The warmth of the sun covered the cemetery like a baby's blanket. Mr. and Mrs. Landry had done a wonderful job setting up for the ceremony. About a hundred chairs lined the grass in neat rows leading back from where Pete was to be buried, and a small podium was placed off to the side. Although they had decided not to hold the funeral in a church, a minister came out to conduct the service. Flowers lined the casket, the podium and the rows of chairs. If it weren't for the fact they were actually in a cemetery, it might have appeared to be a wedding.

"Everything looks wonderful, Mrs. Landry," Hope said as they came up to greet Pete's parents.

"Thank you, dear. We just wanted it to be special for Peter."

"Oh, Cole, that reminds me," Mr. Landry began. "I don't know if you knew this or not, but we own a small house up at Big Bear Mountain. We keep it rented most of the time, but it happens to be vacant right now. Mrs. Landry and I wondered if you and Hope would be interested in taking a couple of days up there before going back down to school. You've been such a good friend to Pete and I am sure you could use a little time away."

"Ah, well, I don't know what to say, Mr. Landry," replied Cole.

"Say 'yes,'" Mr. Landry came back quickly. "It's not much, but the place is fully furnished and it's really nice up there this time of year. The snow season is over and the crowds are gone. It's incredibly peaceful."

"Well, we could definitely use some peace. What do you think, Hopes?" Cole asked.

"I think it sounds fantastic," smiled Hope.

"Then it's settled. I have the directions and the keys in the car. Follow me over and I'll tell you how to get there, Cole," Mr. Landry added. Mrs. Landry watched her husband put his arm around Cole's shoulder and walk with him to the car.

"Hello, Cynthia," She turned to see Ben and Lucy Anderson. "Our hearts are with you and Bill," said Mr. Anderson. "How have you been holding up?"

"I'm holding, but I don't know about how up I am," Mrs. Landry replied.

"Hello, Mr. and Mrs. Anderson." Hope greeted Cole's parents.

"Well, you have certainly done a beautiful job on the decorations, Cynthia," Mrs. Anderson commented.

"Thank you, dear. It's the least we can do for Peter," Mrs. Landry replied.

Hope realized Mrs. Landry was more or less on autopilot. She was calling everyone "dear" and seemed dazed—aware of what was going on, but definitely in her own little world. And who could blame her? She had just lost her son, her only boy, her star athlete, her pride and joy.

It has to be the most difficult challenge for a parent when their child dies. Losing a parent is a shock, but it is pretty well expected that a parent will die before their children. When the situation is reversed and a child dies first, there is nothing that can prepare a parent for that, nothing at all.

There was now a sizeable crowd gathering. Jake and the girls had arrived. Both of Jake's parents were also there, although they sat on opposite sides, and barely spoke two words to Jake and didn't even meet Susan. Most of the baseball team had driven up, including Coach Kowalski, Pete's Coach Numbnuts. Dozens of family friends and local relatives, other childhood friends of Pete's, and even Professor McIntry came to pay their respects.

Cole was really taken back when he saw the professor; he hadn't known Pete other than from what Cole had said about him. This was exactly the sort of thing that made the professor such an incredible person. Cole thought about how much the professor had influenced his life of late—how much he had impacted everyone. Even Pete had benefitted from what they had learned.

As the service started and everyone was in their seats, Cole's mind wandered through the events of the last semester: his former infidelities; Pete's varsity baseball games; Jake's new relationship with Susan; Professor McIntry's great lessons, plus his own private sessions and meditations; Hope's finally breaking free from the influence of her mother's death; and Jake's disappearing stutter. It had been an incredible year and he had incredible friends.

"Now, to give Peter Landry's eulogy," the minister announced, "is his friend of fifteen years, Cole Anderson."

Cole slowly walked up to the podium and cleared his throat. He looked over at the coffin, which sat on metal rods ready to be lowered into the ground, and took a deep breath. Ironically, he felt unusually calm, incredibly calm. He took another deep breath, looked up at the sky, then peered out over the crowd and began to speak.

"Pete was my best friend and he still is. To me, he's not gone. He's just taken on a different role. He was always the one who made sure everything we did turned out to be fun. Now he gets to watch over us to make sure we're all still smiling.

"You always knew exactly when Pete entered a room. If he wasn't raising his hands in the air and declaring his presence, you'd just get the sense that something had changed. He had such an incredible energy; it was rare to see Pete without a smile. He was a constant reminder of how we often get so caught up in our little life dramas that we begin to take ourselves too seriously for our own good. Pete had a way of gently showing us we needed to lighten up. He showed us how precious life is and that we need to make each moment count.

"And Pete did make each moment count. He lived his life without holding anything back, without caring what other people thought and without turning down a challenge. He didn't need to give you a speech or lecture in order to get his point across; he just was. He just was himself. He was so beautifully himself that it inspired us all. I think it is clear how much he inspired us by the number of people here today, many of whom only knew Pete for a short time.

"I will remember his spirit in every smile I see, and with every belly laugh that I have or I hear. I will remember his spirit with every clinking of glasses in a toast made to good friends. I will remember his spirit in every twinkle and shine of the billions of stars that look down and protect us from ourselves. I will remember his spirit in each and every one of you, because you couldn't have known Pete without taking on at least a sliver of his courage, or his laughter, or his compassion. I will remember his spirit in everything I do, feel and say, because my best friend will never leave me. He will always be by my side. He will always be my wingman."

Cole paused and slowly looked around at the faces of Pete's friends and family. Many had half smiles of joyful sadness; most of them were crying, including the baseball team. Looking back over at the coffin, Cole said, "I love you, Pete."

The service wound down and everyone gave their condolences. Many headed back to the Landrys' for post-funeral finger food and heavy drinking.

Hope and Cole said their good-byes to family and friends. They made certain to spend a few minutes talking with Professor McIntry, who said he was deeply touched by the eulogy. They decided they would take off for the cabin right away instead of joining everyone at the Landrys' house. Conversation about Pete's funeral made the two-hour drive seem to go by in no time at all.

When they arrived at the cabin it was already getting dark. They had decided to stay just one night, so they hadn't concerned themselves with extra clothes. They stopped off to pick up a toothbrush, toothpaste, some food for dinner, and a bottle of wine.

They climbed the steps to the front deck and unlocked the door to the cabin. As they walked in, Cole had an immediate sense of *déjà vu*, just like he had the night of Pete's accident. He got a chill all over as he tried to think why everything looked so familiar. What was it? Why did he sense he had been here before? Then, all of a sudden he knew.

"Hopes, remind me to tell you about my meditations," Cole said, smiling.

"Okay." She didn't understand but had decided to agree with him. "I'm starved. I'm going to get the food ready."

"Sounds great! Do you need any help?" Cole asked.

"No, not at all. Thanks though," replied Hope.

"I am going to jump in the shower, okay?" Cole said as he got undressed.

As Cole was getting out of the shower he heard music coming from the main room. "That's great, Hopes. There's a stereo here?" he said.

"Yeah, and it has a CD player as well. Why don't you grab the CDs from the jeep?" Hope suggested.

"Not before I get a kiss," he replied as he put on his shirt. He came up behind her and nibbled on her neck. She turned and gave him a big kiss. As their lips unlocked, she saw him eye the food. She stuck a cracker with cheese in his mouth—to his delight.

When Cole came back in with a handful of CDs he'd retrieved from the car, Hope was sitting on the floor in front of the couch with some appetizers and two glasses of wine. "Honey, you are the best," he said as he walked over to the stereo. "What do you want to listen to?"

"Do we have any U2 in there?" Hope asked.

"This is incredible," he said, laughing to himself. He put in *The Joshua Tree* and sat down next to Hope. "I've got to tell you…this is incredible."

"What? What's incredible?" Hope asked anxiously.

"Okay, well, Professor McIntry taught me how to meditate, right? Just like in class, he said we can actually help create our circumstances. You know, that our reality is shaped by our thoughts. So, he told me about affirmations and to start affirming and visualizing something I wanted to happen." Cole was getting excited, but Hope was still confused as to why.

"I've done it three times a day for the last few weeks, with the exception of the last day or so. Hopes, my affirmation was that we were in a cabin spending a weekend together. I visualized every detail, the mountains, all the trees around…hell, I even visualized U2 playing in the background, and then you just picked it to listen to. Man, this is unbelievable," Cole was talking faster at this point.

"That is incredible. I've been reading a lot about visualization and the power of the mind," Hope said. "The professor's class has really gotten me into it. It's exciting. You think about what you are going to be doing, and then it happens. You know, you're going to have to teach me how to do it."

"Definitely. Yet I know the professor started me out really basic," Cole added. "There's got to be so much more to explore. So much to explore about ourselves." Cole sat there in thought, smiling and looking at Hope with a deep sense of love. Something outside caught Hope's attention. She squinted out the sliding glass door to get a better look. She smiled, then laughed and said, "Cole, look out there, in back. Could it be any more perfect?"

Cole turned to see what Hope was talking about. In the distance was a hammock tied to two trees. Smiling, he turned back around to Hope and asked, "Can dinner wait?"

"It will have to," she replied and they walked outside. They snuggled up side by side in the hammock and looked out over the tops of the trees at the starry night.

"I wish I had gotten to share the magic hammock with Pete; I know he would have liked it," Cole said, gazing into the stars.

Suddenly a shooting star streaked across the sky, just for a moment, then burned out of existence. There was no need for words. They looked at each other and understood each other's thoughts. At times like this they knew everything was going to be all right. At times like this they just knew. What an incredible journey it had been so far. What an incredible journey lay ahead.

BIBLIOGRAPHY

Allen, Woody. Quotation of unknown source.

"The Autobiography of Benjamin Franklin." *The Harvard Classics, 1*. New York: P. F. Collier, 1909.

Epicurus. Quotation from his "Letter to Meoceceus."

Falcone, Giovanni. Quotation. Speech of unknown title.

Fieger, Leslie. *The Delfin Knowledge System* ™. Alexandria Corporation, 1995.

"Fruits of Solitude/William Penn." *The Harvard Classics, 1*. New York: P. F. Collier, 1909.

"The Journal of John Woolman." *The Harvard Classics, 1*. New York: P. F. Collier, 1909.

Julius Caesar. In William Shakespeare. 1623 First Folio. H. H. Furness, Jr., 1913.

Moss, Robert. *Conscious Dreaming.* New York: Crown Publishing, 1996.

Salinger, J. D. *The Catcher in the Rye*. Boston: Little, Brown and Company, Inc., 1951.

Wilde, Stuart. *Whispering Winds of Change*. Hay House Books, 1993.

Give the Gift of
Between Friends
to Your Friends, Colleagues and Students

CHECK YOUR LEADING BOOKSTORE OR ORDER HERE

YES, I want _____ copies of **Between Friends** at $13.95 each, plus $4 shipping per book (Florida residents please add $.84 sales tax per book). International orders must be accompanied by a postal money order in U.S. funds. Include $5.00 for delivery and allow up to 15 days.

My check or money order for $_____ is enclosed.
Please charge my: ❑ Visa   ❑ MasterCard

Name _____

Organization _____

Address _____

City/State/Zip _____

Phone _____

Card # _____

Exp. Date_____   Signature _____

Please make your check payable and return to:
Global Learning Systems, LLC
1314 E. Las Olas Blvd., #15
Fort Lauderdale, FL 33301

Call your credit card order to: 954-522-2696
Fax: 954-522-7092